ONLY ALIVE ON SUNDAYS

ONLY ALIVE ON SUNDAYS

A NOVELLA

KIM RASHIDI

Kim Rashidi explores the cosmos through her words and has a soft spot for capturing love and life in the mundane. Writing about the lives, cities, and timelines that mirror back the romantic, she weaves reality with imagined possibilities. She holds an MA in English literature and is based in Toronto.

Also by Kim Rashidi
Fortunate: Tarot Poetry
GIRL MESS: A Katabasis in Verse

THE MOON.

STRENGTH.

JUDGEMENT.

THE HIGH PRIESTESS.

DEATH.

THE WORLD.

THE DEVIL.

THE MAGICIAN.

TEMPERANCE.

THE STAR.

THE EMPEROR.

JUSTICE.

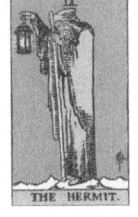
THE HERMIT.

THE HIEROPHANT.

THE LOVERS.

THE SUN.

THE EMPRESS.

THE HANGED MAN.

THE FOOL.

WHEEL of FORTUNE.

THE CHARIOT.

THE TOWER.

"...only someone who has eaten a succulent pear could understand her."

—Clarice Lispector, *An Apprenticeship or The Book of Pleasures* (trans. Stefan Tobler)

I.

THE MOON

Her summer started—but mostly ended—with nothing but tacit glances of love. Maybe it was lust, but she was not one to clarify such things.

A chaotic silence inside the shop brewed—it was the whirling usually associated with an empty home lit up with candles as if in waiting of guests that were forgotten to be invited. The lonely sounds spilled from a tucked-away section with the most antiquated of antiques. It was an ominous invitation which could not be placed because she was in limbo—an act of perpetual waiting. The lack of commotion was synonymous with either a curse or a blessing; though she did not know which one for a fact.

He lived out there, somewhere in the world. He took up space on the train and probably ate at the same restaurants she did. His image poured into her mind—as was typical in waiting games—despite not having seen each other for years. He seemingly did not exist outside of her. He was real in the sense that his materiality had come into contact with hers once, but there was no more to him than a forced memory. She sat there, behind the register of the shop, idled by the thought of him. It was paralyzing—nothing could happen; she missed him.

The cure to the onslaught of memory was clear. She needed to chase away the culprit, replace it with something else, or kill it off entirely. She chose the latter intuitively—her hand drew out letters and shapes she certainly meant but did not intend to voice.

The letter began:

Love letter for—

The chimes above the door did what they were intended to do, alerting her to a tweed coat's entrance.

All Mila could hear was her heart aching like thunder in the sky ready to split open at the thought of something electric on the precipice. It would be an invocation she did not truly mean: that she'd started writing a letter to him, and there he'd be.

But, it was not *him*. His face was ambiguous these days, and his motivation for dropping by her workplace— not very high. He would likely do anything to avoid crossing paths. He would also never wear tweed. The similarities between the two men were perhaps energetic and only mildly physical. Timelines were warping—for how could the similarity be so present and absent, she thought. Either that, or she had tricked herself in noticing *him* in everyone else.

The Tweed approached her, eyeing the beginning of her written confession. A half-smile escaped him before he spoke—he seemed pleased that she was writing a love letter.

"I was here yesterday, reading in the back corner. I believe I left something I intended to purchase."

He mouthed the word *intended* as suspiciously as humanly possible, she thought.

She had not noticed him yesterday. Perhaps he had seemed invisible to her in the crowd of patrons on a Saturday, the busiest day of all, as they searched for a bump—a reunion with the divine.

"Maybe I can help you find it again. There's only been a couple of people in today, and I doubt they would have picked it up. What was it?" she asked.

"That would be lovely. I appreciate your help," he said, "It's a leather-bound journal with the initials J.M. on it."

She thought it over in her mind. She left her place

behind the counter to join him in the main room of the shop to have some fun.

"The one with the gold-string bookmark?"

"Yes! That would be the one," he said, seeming overjoyed but somehow remaining composed.

She wondered how he got here, what the journal had professed to him, what sort of string it had pulled on his heart. The temptation to tease The Tweed, to perhaps coax it out of him, settled in.

"Oh yeah, we sent that back to the warehouse. We thought it useless," she said.

He let out a gentle huff, tasking her with reading his subtle emotion.

"Well, how can I retrieve it? It looked like the one my grandfather kept in his study when I was younger, and I need to purchase it."

She brightened, a sparkle in her eye almost glistened as he revealed the tip of the iceberg.

"Sorry, were you sitting in the back right corner, or the left? Where did you find the journal?" she inquired, as if it would make a difference.

"What is the difference? I found it and I intend to buy it," he said, bluntly.

She said nothing, and yet, she begged silence to cooperate and be as unbearable as it sometimes is just so The Tweed could nervously fill, with words, the horror of staring at a stranger in anticipation of conversation.

"Fine," he said, "Back left. The section of antiques labelled *portal*."

She smiled gently, accepting his defeat—though internally, she was brimming with satisfaction.

"I am afraid you can't purchase it then," she responded, knowing he would prompt further given how desperate he seemed for something to tie him to his bloodline.

This was as good a time as any for Mila to notice the pristineness of The Tweed—both the coat and the man. His hair—delicately combed—and his shoes—without scuffs. Even the beauty marking his face was completely symmetrical. She was sure he was measured to be just as he is. This is not a man of coincidences, she thought, so how could he have forgotten the journal so beloved to him?

"And may I ask why not?" he asked, simply, calmly, instinctively.

"Like you so eloquently said," and she almost called him Tweed here, but refrained *despite* being a girl of coincidences, "it's from the portal section. The items there are always personal and always a reflection of the visitor. You can purchase them at the time of encounter, or they will be gone—back into the portal."

A raise of the eyebrow! A rare sighting for The Tweed, Mila assumed.

"What do you take me for?" he asked, a little annoyed.

"Go and look again, you'll find something else to tie you over, and this time, you can act on your intention to buy it," she said, smugly.

He opened his mouth to speak, as if to argue with the girl working at an antique shop claiming that the store was magical. But he settled for a simple nod and began his extremely neat stride toward the portal section. Having the burden of explaining the situation relieved of her, Mila began making a cup of coffee for The Tweed. Surely he would need it after finding something that would confirm the reality of the shop.

*

When she came across Luna Antiques a few years ago, Mila couldn't comprehend it either. She had encountered a deck of cards, intricately decorated with small fruits and cloaks of luxury. It had been a gift from her mother at the tiny age of sixteen. The deck, however, had gone missing just recently then. Seeing it at the shop, she had known it was her deck: the back of the first card, the elusive card zero, was signed with a note from her mother: *Here's to the journey.* With the cards, she had learned a new language with which to encounter the world—always in search of meaning, something to make the mundane magical. Finding it again had to be a sign, she thought.

The girl who ran the shop back then was just as mysterious as its functionality. She was ethereal, in the most calming sense of the word. She watched Mila scour the day's curiosities in the portal section—and that was an initiation neither of them had yet figured out. When Mila had taken over the shop, she did not realize she would witness the slippery joy of a patron finding a piece of themselves on the back shelf of an antique store. She also did not realize how draining it would be to facilitate connections with the past. Mila had taken her new post without much discernment—she would be there every single day making coffee to comfort a crying grandmother or to ease the anxiety of a man who has never before expressed how much it means to him to be a part of something bigger, to be part of a delicate series of events all interwoven into the present moment.

*

She set The Tweed's coffee down on the table closest to the portal section—an intimately intoxicating section of the shop, one which induced states of being not unlike learning new words for feelings one did not know existed—and told him she would be at the counter if he wanted her to ring him out. He was handling a few things Mila didn't take him to be the type for: a quartz crystal in one hand, Polaroids and letters initialed with red lipstick in the other. She wanted to linger longer, to read over his shoulder, but she remembered she had her own letter to get back to.

Deciding to leave the name blank, *love letter for whomever*—but with a very specific person in mind—she started again:

> *Tonight is a full moon, you know? I have spent years thinking of how you spend your days, your nights, the moments in between dreams. I wanted to know if you were okay, in love, fighting your demons, or simply having fun. Tonight is a full moon, and so I am wrought with the temptation of closing out this chapter—with you, specifically, but with the numbing pain of yearning, generally.*

"Pardon," The Tweed said.

The warm depth of his voice triggered Mila's romantic eyeing of the situation. His words echoed with certainty long after he was finished speaking. She followed their lead while keeping her pen in hand but leaving the letter open faced and exposed as if to allow the words to marinate.

"Yes?" she said, approaching him.

Beside him, leaning on the back wall of the poorly-lit portal section, there was a mirror with a frame of golden flowers. The reflection was sobering—a blazing sun worthy of a summer spent by the shore with blueberries in hand—plopped into insatiable mouths, staining fingertips a violet colour unbeknownst to flesh except when in rotting.

The Tweed picked up the mirror, examining it with blatant casualness. That was peculiar. People almost always had a look of utmost disbelief, and sometimes relief, on their face. They always saw the dots connect. But for The Tweed, the juice of sun rays dripping off the frame signified nothing but time off from his teaching or research in ancient literature, or so Mila assumed having glanced at his eyes through his glasses.

"May I enquire about the price of this piece?" he asked, remaining distant as if it had no relation to him.

Mila wondered what the mirror was a placeholder for in his life. Could it be a literal reflection of his pain? Would he find the shape of his mother's eyes in himself when looking at it, through it? She wanted to ask him all the questions popping into her mind as if they were spam emails arriving in an inbox, but she had learned better than to pry in on the lives of the patrons. She once asked a Newsboy Cap about the tea cup with a chihuahua painted on it, and they offered no real story at all but an extravagant tale of a childhood goldfish that had taken to the neighbour's dog. The story made no sense at all.

"Whatever is in your left pocket, that's the price," she informed The Tweed.

"Let me see," he said while fishing with his veiny hand into the depths of his pocket.

He presented his open palm to her with the contents of his pocket laid atop it.

"I have a ten, a card for the bookshop down the street, which, by the way, could have a better coffee maker or at least some wine, and the key to my mailbox."

She received the contents of his pocket into her own hand. She had never heard of the purported bookshop down the street from Luna, but its card was familiar. A cloudy background with three swords piercing a levitating heart. She knew the image as if it was her first uttered word—it dangled meaning over their heads, though she did not notice if it was intended for herself or for him. She did, however, notice how off-putting a symbol it was for a bookshop.

She accepted the card, flipping it over to find the address of the store. She slid it into her pocket, placed the cash into the register, and handed the key back to The Tweed.

"You can keep that, unless you don't get mail. You get mail, right?" she asked.

"Yes, I get mail," he said, with an air of perceived flirtation.

Leave it to a teacher to flirt about getting mail, Mila thought.

"Okay, then keep it. And enjoy your mirror, I guess."

"It's not a mirror," he replied.

She looked at him to prompt further explanation.

He gave in like before, setting the pace for how they interact.

"My grandfather painted this when he was only 24 years old."

As if his grandfather's age was the significant part of the painting, she thought. Mila held his eyes for a moment to imply as much. He held it right back, not budging this time—likely because he had no adequate answer himself.

She brushed it off and looked at the mirror again. He was right, the thing blared with the light of the sun but was not actually reflecting anything at all. A clear sky was present in the painting, and turning her eyes to the clouds settling into the sky outside, she decided to believe him.

The Tweed expressed his gratitude earnestly, though his presence lingered longer than would be typically acceptable. They held each other's gaze, one tempting the other to say something more. Though neither did.

The Tweed picked up the painting and exited the shop—the sound of chimes bookended his second visit to Luna Antiques. His smile, she now noticed, was a little tilted to one side, ingrained itself into her mind and it felt as though there had been a spot for its memory there all along.

Mila returned to her letter:

Only Alive on Sundays

I can't seem to loosen my grip on the idea of you in my life, and sometimes, it's you who I think needs to do the growing, but maybe it's the idea of you that I need to grow out of. Maybe I need to learn a little bit more about the world to better understand you when you disappear...What a romantic I am to call this love. Perhaps the reason I call this a love letter instead of anything else is a deep knowing that I can't even wrap my head around. I call this a love letter because I do love you, but not in the way people traditionally do. I love you like I love Sundays. I can anticipate them when the days cycle Monday through Saturday. I tolerate the days in between because I know there's a Sunday to come back to. I love you because I anticipate you. The truth is, I have no idea the type of life you live or anything about you, really. I am basing my love on snippets I have gathered based on what you have said and shared so limitedly. I am afraid to admit that the way I know you, so intimately in my mind, is a fantasy. But it's a full moon, you know, and who would I be if I didn't take the time to appreciate that I can love at all?

It hurts to know you like this, but most half-known things do. I hope to know you, really know you, or forget you completely.

Until then, yours in keeping,
Mila

She took the letter, put it in an envelope, walked over to the portal section, and behind a shattered—yet mended—golden plate, she dropped it into a letter slot labelled "the ether."

Perhaps she had done it once and for all. She hoped that the letter would kill him off as if he were a character in the show of her life.

II.

STRENGTH

In the mirror, Mila eyed her reflection and the reversed image of her blue-tiled bathroom. She considered the blue—a baby, yet pungent one. It was rather melancholic—it had an air of outside, but was decidedly an inside colour. It was the blue of the sky some mornings: undisturbed by clouds and the loudness of humans existing. It was the blue a heaven would be, if there were one at all. The melancholy was partly nostalgic. Mila considered that this is the type of blue rarely witnessed in its natural form—hence an inside colour—it is one manufactured by a company on some street to make people feel something, to sell tiles. It's typically bought to pretend the owner wakes up feeling whole, or to pretend they are a fairy during the little light morning offers before the sun rises; the two feelings are indistinguishably the same.

*

When she had toured the apartment, Mila only somewhat liked the layout. She had been able to imagine herself reading in one corner or another, she had liked the kitchen—its wooden white cupboards, the old-timey fridge, the island overlooking the living room. The thing she had liked most was the blue in the bathroom; it had invoked a sense of belonging in her that she never knew well enough to recognize. It had been the blue tiles that chose her instead of her choosing them, or the apartment at that. She had also liked the phone booth right outside the front door for no particular reason. The phone in the booth was near its expiration date—its rings crescendoed each time an inhabitant exited the building, but she had liked it anyway. It had reminded her of the subtlety of change, of how days pass by all seemingly the same, but with small alterations that eventually lead to a big one.

*

Splashing her face with water, Mila already felt awake—despite the gloom beyond her blue-tiled bathroom. She took the morning to tend to the plants overflowing out of most rooms of her apartment. She sang them a song of growth and wished them a good day. Her plants were up to good most days—she knew that for certain.

A week had passed since her encounter with The Tweed, and she had only thought of him once. It was the look of his hands reaching into his pocket that had tricked her psyche into wanting to see him again—and his smile probably played a role in that, too.

She should have gone to open the shop, but something in her wanted to savour the morning a bit longer—*and* it was Sunday. Rarely did she fully enjoy the day she loved most. So, she decided a late start would harm no one at all.

Melting into a velveteen loveseat—notably named for conversing with the one one wishes to know more deeply—she fingered at the pages of various magazines. Reading is like gathering bits of information meaningful only to one's self—to speak of at a later time with those who share the same fundamental beliefs about living—she thought.

She took out her favourite mug—one she'd made and glazed at a pottery class just before she had met *him*. It was uneven in all the right places with its shapely curves and poised lips, its checkered pink, and its purple interior—she had brought it to life start to finish, and now, it, and its contained liquid, brought her to life every morning.

The aroma of freshly made coffee was flowing about in her apartment leaving specks of golden brown in the air. Mila was sure the smell was permeating the walls into the neighbours' homes. It delighted her to think that those very same specks fell right into the noses of humans living just past her walls and brought them out of the depths of sleep, their eyes slowly batting open to find a new day presented to them. Not a clean slate exactly, but something along those lines. She fell curious to their routines, to their awakening on Sundays. She wanted to sniff out the smells emanating from their homes as if they were apparitions of a life lived that could walk through walls—but she had other vices and virtues to tend to first.

She could have blamed the earliness with which she had awoken on the gloom outside—not entirely gloom, just day without sun—but she decided to wait it out. And within an hour, the sun made a glorious return to the day sky, and the baby blue was a perfect match to her tiles just for the time being. She was learning time was essential. Mila thought to herself that she ought to wait until later every day to open the shop. The mornings were too precious to not spend at home, in peace, worshipping a love that exists between sheets and magazines with delectable lines of poetry.

Mila was on her third magazine of the morning, this one filled with the romance of bodies of water—all in flirtation with land and sun—when via her mail slot, a piece of paper took flight into her home. A sun ray was hitting the exact direction with which the letter would enter, and so a natural spotlight was put onto its dance, an erotic one with its many twists of shape and almost audibly perceptible *whoosh* of space breaking. She glanced at the ruse demanding her attention and gave it just that. Perhaps the paper was a notice of some sort, but a building notice would not dance so seductively, and she knew while walking toward the front door and then bending down to pick up the paper gracing her floor that this was in fact a response—either from him or the ether.

The letter was short and simple, but lacking the sweetness typically associated with the first two adjectives:

Get over it.

It was signed rather insincerely: *the ether.*

She was almost in shock, but she knew the ether had a knack for hard truths; and the letter from last week was, admittedly, the third one she had sent this season. Perhaps there was some truth to the ether's imploring that she "get over it." A response was nonetheless better than nothing at all.

After a hard stare at the letter, while dust particles danced in her home disturbed by the foreignness of the paper, she decided that today, she *would* get over it. Mila considered how delicious it would be to not dedicate so much energy to someone who barely acknowledges her existence. But how does one, so in routine with daily longing and romance, just fall out of a distant love they pursued for their own pleasure, she questioned.

He was indeed loved by her but, of course, not in the typical sense of the word. He was loved by her like one loves a stranger in the wild who, by the way, has luscious hair that imitates the waves of an ocean *and* happens to be reading a book that is particularly meaningful to the onlooker. But she also loved him for how he made her love herself, and she thought that was rare. And although they hadn't spoken in months—his preferred method of keeping her at bay being a text here or there—wasn't it worth it to have love for someone that left space for magic in her life? He left the aforementioned space simply by existing as someone who knows the intimacies of her mind, she thought.

Mila knew at this moment that she so-called *loved* him because he had at one point made her feel seen. But that was no longer the case. In fact, he now made her feel

Only Alive on Sundays

invisible. If she couldn't interact with him—him, who lives not far at all—was *she* even real? She had no answer. Questions and realizations are not exactly an answer to soothe rabid minds and hearts. It's not as if she can just get over it with ease. Though, the letter did not indicate easiness. Mila knew not of resistance in situations such as these, and she knew love in a different face would welcome her soon enough if she could just figure out how to properly deal with the displaced tragedy of her current predicament.

Taking a break from the monstrous task of getting over it, Mila changed into a dress made solely for the summer and went down to the fruit market in the square close to her home. The journey over was not consumed by thoughts as she imagined it might be, rather it was simple, easy, even sweet. The air was light and the sky, comforting—as they should be. She asked the sky what all this was for, what learning is there to do when you're in the thick of yearning marked by chapters of *short love*? The sky had no answer, but Mila made out a chuckle from the lips formed by clouds. Maybe *short love* was the truest love—in passing, and always with minimal expectations, a brief moment of answering just to the heart.

Mila had her head held up to the clouds when she felt taps at her toes—apples and oranges rolled at her feet. She looked down to find a girl picking them up.

"Sorry," the girl said, looking up at Mila.

Mila knelt down to help her with the fruits, both exchanging a smile—currency for a day spent feeling alright. She placed them delicately in the tote bag the girl was carrying. *Short love*, Mila confirmed.

Examining the zucchinis, cherry tomatoes, oyster mushrooms, and other much smaller vegetables just with her eyes, Mila concocted a recipe for lunch and gathered all her materials slowly. She grazed the vegetables with a light hand, tracing their outline, appreciating their dance of stillness, their acts of meditation. She felt a keen appreciation for the freshness life was offering her today, and to waste that would be a mistake. She knew! Then why was there an inkling in her throat, begging her to settle back into the comfort of wanting something she couldn't have?

She walked around the stands, all a little magical under the sun—the light laid itself upon earth with a soft glow and was accompanied by the sounds of people in a choir of purchase. She was moving with less attention to her surroundings and was now deeper in thought than she would have liked. The excursion was meant to be a break from the stickiness of whatever love she felt, but the more lax she got with the idea of love and how she tucks it into her metaphorical pockets, the stickier *it* got. It oozed into her thoughts, and perhaps reality. Sticky hands were everywhere, leaving fingerprints to chase and hold accountable for whatever sap was left over after nights of honeyed thoughts.

Love, she decided, is a hunt—it is an energy that people put out almost like a spider weaving its web; it feeds humans their own memories caught in bloodlust. The blood of love seeps out from eyes like the juice of sweet nectarines—it drips down throats, chests, spines—a reminder that love is the deed of the living, always messy and an indication of desire as a sticky form of suffering.

Once again, Mila knew time was what she needed, more time with love, not in the typical sense, but love as in a moment of joy that feels like a good stretch after a night's sleep in bodily positions not meant for the human form. She had let the pit of conversations had with him keep her going and keep her in love with life, but she decided it wasn't him who her love was for.

And as if speaking of the devil, there *he* was at the fruit market just three blocks from her house buying fruits like nothing had ever happened. Nothing *had* ever happened—but how was it that the person she was just

Only Alive on Sundays

thinking of appeared right there and was feeling out a mango, a peach, a plum?

She watched from a distance as his hands made love to the fruits—only through her eyes, of course. To the regular market shopper, he was examining the fruits. She wanted more than anything to catch his eye, to wave hello, to tap his shoulder, give him a smile. Desiring him was how she spent half her days and she considered that his physical intrusion was perhaps the universe's way of giving her a taste of whatever she calls this torment.

Decidedly, Mila started in his direction, planning out a route and a conversation that would be seamless, easy.

And then she stopped.

She could not, would not, "get over it" like this. She looked at him—him who was unaware of the situation—and she wanted to know which fruits he liked most, what he'd make for lunch, or since when he'd started coming to the market. But she knew she did not need to know any of these things.

Feeling sucked into the potential encounter, she was stuck standing in the middle of the market. Mila was blocking the most proper route, so people passed her by going around her. Someone even knocked into her, bumping out a sigh that, thankfully, brought her back to the moment—she let go of whatever conversation was possible.

She turned her attention to an array of books at the market—their covers wore yellow hues that matched her dress. Eyes fell upon her skin softly, warmly like the sun. She looked up to find The Tweed radiating a look at her from the other side of table. He nodded at Mila in faux recognition and offered a full smile before he could muffle his excitement for seeing her. She smiled back, waiting for him to break the quiet barrier in between them.

"Thanks for letting me keep the mail key yesterday. I received an immensely important letter today," he said, emphasizing the word immensely as if it was a joke.

She knew he was serious and was confused on how to answer. She picked up a play about witches and returned her gaze to him.

"No problem at all," she said, remembering she had also gotten an "immensely important letter" today.

"Any good news in that letter of yours?" she pried.

It was The Tweed's turn to be taken aback by Mila's casualness.

"You could say that."

He grappled with silence for a moment, averting his eyes down to the array of books, then to the market surrounding them, and back to her inquisitive eyes.

"That's a good play," he said, nodding toward the book she had picked up.

She said nothing, knowing he was avoiding the question. She gave him the space to express himself.

He seemed to jump into words, seemingly convincing himself that he had nothing to lose. Thrilled, he started to tell her that he'd written himself a letter years and years ago and had asked a friend to mail it to him on this day, his birthday.

"I had forgotten all about it, and suddenly received it today! It certainly changed my life. The rest of it anyway."

He realized that he had perhaps shared too much and slightly recoiled, but Mila took the smile that slipped off his lips and wore it for him.

"Happy birthday," she said, somewhat detached in her attempt to contain her happiness for him and the similarity she had just witnessed. Birthday letters were her thing, too.

Mila noticed him relax, she assumed he felt an ease in their conversation, like there was nothing in the way of their ability to be honest with each other despite their limited interactions.

"Hey, would you like to come to my party? I live not too far and it's been a while since I've thrown a party—I'm well stocked I think, if that piques your interest."

She took a moment to consider and glanced over at *him* still at the market, still picking out the week's groceries. She decided she would go. She would go and get over it.

"Sure, which street are you on?" she asked.

He gave her the address, "See you tonight."

She nodded an implied *see you there* and imagined the night misted with mystery and music that spills onto streets, she imagined string lights decorating whatever outdoor patio The Tweed surely had, and she imagined herself amongst a crowd she knew nothing of. The Tweed nodded back and they once again held each other's eyes as if mutually understanding something, but neither were clear on what. He looked away first, she still held her eyes on him as he made his way toward some other stand eerily close to *him*.

The two men seemed to exchange a word or two about the produce, and to her own disbelief, she did nothing. She watched them interact, feeling giddy about their exchange of energy. She jokingly wondered if *he* was now invited to the party, too. She watched them in awe for a moment and felt herself being called to go home—to make lunch with all the ingredients she had bought and the ones she did not, to go into the meal to be consumed and digested. It would be a spell to un-become a story she had fed herself.

III.

(CLOUDED) JUDGEMENT

The portal section hummed with its gaping mouth—an indication of the life it leads all on its own. Mila knew the sound to be a beckoning to tend to its altar, to tidy it in gratitude of its servitude between the mortal realm and the universe. She did not completely understand how the letter slot acted as the connective material—the materialization of ideas amongst the worlds—so she made up her own reason to understand the peculiarity of both the shop and the life she was living at present. Maybe it had always been like this, all throughout time, a channel of some sort pulling down what needs to be heard for the parameters of the universe to expand as it wishes to. Maybe the universe had caught up with technology but wished to stay away from it. Maybe a mail slot was its preferred technology due to its genuine anonymity or, maybe, it was a symbol that meaning can materialize just about anywhere, *if* one is seeking the aforementioned meaning.

    Mila began with a damp wipe across the humble shelf—empty with its lack of patrons, save herself. She wondered why her presence did not secure a constant overflowing of nostalgic paraphernalia, or rather ephemera, [*Brief-lasting a short time*] which should hold no meaning at all except to mark time. But memory, as with habit, is imbued with so much meaning that living in the present is hardly a possibility, she thought. Perhaps the emptiness—nothingness—was of significance, too.

    She closed the opening flap of the slot with slight pressure to ensure its closure—her own, too—and felt resistance. *It* was pushing back. Mila thought it was to tease

Only Alive on Sundays

her, and she wondered what this scene looked like to an outsider. If there were a hidden camera somewhere, projecting her life at this very moment to a group of unknown strangers—or worse, to a group of scientists studying human nature—would they enjoy the scene? Be on the edge of their seats? They must be on some high-horse, she thought, sending letters to fool humans into trusting some all-knowing presence, letting it guide their life to convince them it was not small, that it meant more, because it must. Either way, experiment or not, Mila had to go on with her mundanities, no matter how long in duration they stretched. She was familiar with the rare experience of being engaged with the most boring of tasks yet still feeling a sense of excitement—for she was alive, and to be alive is to be consumed by one thing or another at any given time. To be consumed by thought, by love, by grief, by greed, or to be the one consuming—consuming people, books, or feasts.

 Mila cleared her mind of the thought, for the observer is always a part of the universe they're observing[1]. It would be of utter dis-use to create such an experiment. Nonetheless, the thought lingered—all the world's a stage[2], and so performativity is at least a part of existence. What else would having a physical form be for? Mila did not know if she liked this thought or not, but she knew *she* was consumed by it entirely. All the times she left her home with the hope of bumping into him, was she not performing in some way, imagining what she looked like from across the street just in case he was there? Was she not trapping him within her, making him real through potentiality? Watching her own life unravel in short bursts of appearance through his eyes? Was she not making a cameo on the stage of her own life—on the TV inside her mind that constantly plays out dramatic scenes just to appease the *him* within?

 Mila eased the tension of her hand on the flap and a new letter poked its body into Luna Antiques. A *whoosh* was its birthing cry—it was unlike the others she had received from the ether. She felt frightened for what it would hold within its folded sticky sides. Would it drip a profession of love through a voice reading exactly what she would have wanted to hear just last week? She knew she was somehow changed by the morning's events. She would just need to face the reality of things being different now.

Unfolding the new letter, she sensed the smell of vague aspirations—if that had a smell at all. It transported her to a faint memory like a madeleine taking a man to childhood—a time of vulnerability. The letter encapsulated her with his scent, enchantingly similar to false hope—maybe pine—it grew stronger with each crease flattening out. It wafted into the shop, took shape like a purple-yellow aura around itself and Mila. But the letter was bare, and the ether was not here to rustle her feathers. She guessed what this meant. For a change, *he* was thinking about *her*. The truth was that she still cared, and to know he thought of her was like fuel. It was a fruit she could devour with haste and deliberate hunger. She cared for her own change of heart, too, but neither held more weight than the other.

But was he thinking positively or negatively of her?

She thought about sending him a letter, like they were long-lost pen pals and not two people living within half an hour of each other. The morning's letter now felt like a premonition, a forewarning to "get over it," despite what happens next. The beliefs one holds on to, Mila thought, should always be accompanied by a despite[3]—one should remain soft and in love despite being shown heartbreak. One should howl under the light of the moon despite its tendency to show up half or full.

Nervously, she fiddled with the straps of her bag at The Tweed's front door. Mila hadn't bothered to change out of the dress from this morning, but it still held shape

Only Alive on Sundays

and graced her skin decoratively despite the day's sun and consequential sweat. Solace from the heat was an escape she was grateful to Luna for—there was always a perpetual flow of air flying about. Thinking about the shop's chill at the front step of The Tweed's door—combined with the cool kiss of the night's wind—was enough to give rise to goosebumps on her skin.

Knocking once more, a little louder, the door pulled open before she could swing her knuckles to it a second time.

It was none other than *him*.

Her intuition from the morning was playing a not-so-funny prank on her, she thought.

"Hi," he said.

"How are you?" she asked, downsizing a smile because the truth was that the excitement was unbearable.

She had *finally* ran into him without any effort on her part. How lucky a feat.

The Tweed grabbed him by the shoulder, a little too generous with the pressure—perhaps due to his superfluous cup of beer.

"Mila! I see you've met..." The Tweed trailed off, looking at him in the shock horror of not remembering his name.

"Baz," he said, offering a gentle smile to ease The Tweed's worrisome expression.

Mila was absolutely amazed by this interaction: how The Tweed had let down his apparent guard, how angelic Baz seemed in the moment for having been wronged by a lapse of memory. It was good for her to know that they *had* just met and were not some lifetime acquaintances. That would be more than she could handle today. Although, they *did* look like formidable school friends with their arms around each other. They seemed more affectionate than she had considered either of them to be—despite her limited knowledge of either's relationship with intimacy, and platonic ones at that.

The three of them stood there for what felt like an eternity—her on the outside of the threshold and the two men on the inside, holding the sort of energy people typically do when they are sure they have the best version of their life possible. The two of them nearly shared the exact same smile. They had been indulging in a bromance of sorts, Mila assumed—they had probably hit it off after she left the market. Maybe Baz had arrived early to the party, bringing in beer to help out The Tweed—who did not look like much of a beer drinker but was nonetheless drinking beer very light-handedly, whereas Baz had the firmest grip on his bottle. He balanced out the neatness with which she imagined The Tweed to live by.

This blue of Baz's shirt was not the same as the tiles in Mila's bathroom. This blue was deep, dark, oceanic in the most intimidating way possible. It held hues of the unknown, the subtlety of getting lost in a new city with no map or phone. His shirt matched what she knew of him, which was not much at all, but his smile and glowing expression were new. She realized she had never seen him in a setting like this—or in many other settings, actually.

Snapping back into reality, Mila answered The Tweed's inquiry, "Yes, we've met. I wish I had known you drink beer. I brought a bottle of wine for you," she said, extending her gift bag to The Tweed.

The Tweed smiled, knowingly, and took the gift with a much too lingering hand on hers. Then, the two men's embrace broke open like a sea parting for a miracle to happen, and she entered, passing the threshold physically, but feeling like an intruder nonetheless. She passed between them, feeling curious of their secrets—if they had any at all. She felt herself jealous of The Tweed, of how Baz had befriended him so naturally. But instead of questioning it, she got over it.

She got over it by lighting a joint on the back patio which was gently lit with bulky string lights taking the shape of miniature lanterns. It was just as she had imagined.

Weighing her options to stay and mingle, talk to Baz and The Tweed—and his wonky smile that had become ridiculously charming due to his inebriation level—or to enjoy solitude tonight, her chest sank with the inability to make a decision. She thought she would need a firm grasp on one answer or another, but blowing out her first inhale's sweet taste, she decided to go where the night took her. No forced interactions, no backing away just to appease the ether or her own desires. The night, she decided, would unfold naturally—a reversal of an origami swan created by time's cruel embrace on inklings of beginnings abandoned half-way.

IV.

THE *HIGH* PRIESTESS

Mila had lazily melted into the couch in the corner but was still buzzing with energy to do something, to be something, to hear what everyone else was saying. This couch was not velveteen like hers, but a more sticky, leathery one. Her dress was long enough to not shoulder the uncomfortable mess of a damp puddle between skin and furniture on a hot summer night. And from her place of rest, she watched some guests swirl out the front door with a curiosity afforded to those who promise that the night shall go on. Though she had taken solace in the couch at present, this was not how she spent the entire night.

*

Mila had played an insidious round of a card game whose name escaped her mind shortly after its end. She had not won as she would've liked to, but she had had fun. Mila had also explored the rooms of The Tweed's home—neat, as would be expected, but his bathroom, namely the forest green tiling, was of surprise. The tiles had landed curiously on Mila. They were too dark a green to induce a sense of immediate passion—it was rather a slow build. She had walked the perimeter of the large bathroom, her hand following the path of her shadow across the tiles. They wore a deeper colour—one reserved for moss, or kelp at the bottom of the ocean. They felt god-like, like a warning, though enveloping at the same time. She had seen herself wrapped by the arms or branches of a tree. Her stomach had grown toasty while she listened to the quiet of a green that the earth was born out of. It was home—in the most displaced sense of the term. This bathroom might as well be a portal itself, into the unknown spectacle of the universe, Mila had thought.

"I like your bathroom tiles," she had informed him as he was torso-deep in his freezer searching for the last remnants of ice.

"You're the second person to say that," he had noted, "Baz was also taken by them."

After a short conversation about his choice in tiles—custom done by himself—and while still shaking the sentiment of Baz being *taken by* bathroom tiling, Mila had asked The Tweed if he'd had a good birthday.

"I thoroughly enjoyed it," he'd said.

He was about to express the highlights of his day and the party when Baz had approached the duo.

"Jakob, I may or may not need a change of clothes. I slipped into the hot tub," he had said, putting emphasis on his wet shirt with a heavy-handed gesturing towards his body.

For once, Mila had been good at hiding her affectionate eyes. Though it had felt like a game of cat and mouse—her eyes following him as a form of betrayal to herself—the desire to examine Baz in his drenched form, with his oh-so unforgivingly translucent shirt, had been overwhelmingly heart-wrenching. Mila had imagined her raw heart in her chest, beating with more excitement than she had known a man on a Sunday to bring her. Had she not been drinking, she may have been able to escape the moment's heat. With a lingering glance and determination settling in, she had turned her eyes to *Jakob*—an odd name for The Tweed. His forehead had been layered by a twofold glistening shield of sweat: he had likely been overjoyed by the events of his party, how smoothly the night had gone, and he had likely also been warm with how easily a home filled with bodies moving about—reaching out for drinks and mouths—could raise the temperature so exorbitantly.

"Could you grab a change of clothes from my bedroom upstairs, Mila? Baz, you can go to the laundry room just off the bathroom here and dump your stuff in the dryer. How's that?" ~~The Tweed~~ Jakob had said so naturally that both were stunned by his direction-giving skills.

They had stood there a moment, frozen by Jakob's bluntness. Perhaps it was his inner teacher coming out, disciplining the misbehaving children, Mila had considered, maybe he was always meant to be a Tweed, maybe he was drunk.

"Yes, boss," Mila had said, to which Baz had chuckled, knotting whichever nerves she had managed to loosen by now.

They had scurried around Jakob's home carrying out their respective tasks. A mischievous grin sparked up both of their faces while fulfilling their duties. Mila was ordered to snoop around—which she had taken her time with, leaving Baz without clothes in the bathroom downstairs, either intentionally or out of a benevolent desire to tease him. Baz's smile was afforded to his slight embarrassment and uncertainty of the situation—if she had wanted to, Mila *could* have abandoned the task entirely. Despite the humour that would have ensued, Mila had delivered the spare change of clothes after an appropriate amount of time—she had knocked at the door and immediately disappeared into the backyard for some air, a delicacy at any party such as this.

*

It was exhilarating for Mila to watch Baz interact with others. She considered his movements while still taking residence on the couch—she had only ever interacted with him one-on-one at misshapen run-ins at local events and conversations through text. Admittedly, she liked the reversal of the roles. She was no longer in her head about how she would look to him. Instead, she was too busy watching words slip out of his mouth with the unrehearsed charm of lips expelling sounds that were drowned out by a busy room. Baz made The Tweed's—Jakob's—intentionality seem practiced, but that was nothing more than contrast. If anything, it made them more similar—they had the same effect through completely different routes. Baz's intentionality was, of course, not intentional. It appeared so to Mila because she had glazed a softness over him that was not entirely his own, but, rather, her projection of him. It was not a pedestal as one would imagine, but, rather, an inner soft-spot poignantly reserved for one person at a time, and it had been his all along without her ever realizing that the seat could not be given to anyone else as long as Baz had a claim on it.

"Hey, you're looking very stoic," Jakob said, joining her on the couch and interrupting her thinking.

"Oh, I am just thinking…who holds a party on a Sunday night? You know people have jobs to get to in the morning, right?" she replied smugly.

Jakob's smile, despite being small, filled the room. The energy immediately turned from the dead of night into the liveliness of the last day of a daunting week—Sunday, seemingly always an inauguration filled with the freedom of a fresh week to start anew. His smile is magic, no, contagious, she thought.

"I wouldn't know. School's out and this teacher is doing absolutely nothing but wandering into weird shops in town," he teased.

Mila knew she could sniff out a Tweed anywhere—not that she was particularly drawn to them. She was simply prone to noticing a singular quality about someone and following through on that thread to assume their insights, their ways of being, the colour of their bathroom tiles.

"Well, some weird shops have to open bright and early on Monday mornings," she mocked back with the exact same look on Jakob's face.

It pleased Mila how a Tweed can turn into a Jakob, with just a few interactions, a mutual acquaintance and a glimpse into his bathroom—his soul, too. *And* through his grandfather's painting. She wondered where it was, why he was keeping it hidden at the party. Perhaps the threat of a group of people talking, moving their bodies and heads in succession to hear one another over the music, was overwhelming for Jakob. Perhaps he had placed it somewhere no person, Mila being the nosiest of them all, would wander.

"I am not sure how many people need antiques and a frenzy of emotions accompanied by said antiquities, but hey, you know your clientele best," he teased once again.

"Well, apparently you did," she said, raising her eyebrow.

"You're right, I did. That painting is really unique, thank you," he said gently.

"You can thank me by offering me a tall glass of water."

"Better yet, how about I thank you with an invitation to wind down in the hot tub?" he asked, to which she perked up.

If there was anything Mila loved, it was being enveloped by bodies of water, no matter hot or cold. Easing from air into water is the most juvenile form of magic, she thought, and with other people, it is a bonding spell of sorts.

Jakob spotted Baz putting on his shoes to leave with the last group of people and called over to him.

"Hey Baz, we're about to hop into the hot tub. I know you already took a dip, but join us," he said, partially dropping his command on language.

She was excited by the prospect but was more curious about Jakob's demeanour. Mila peered at Baz to gauge if he had noticed Jakob's speech to be off. He gave no sense of recognition or answer—he seemingly did not register the secret language Mila was offering. Perhaps he

Only Alive on Sundays

did, and he, too, was preoccupied with the prospect. The tension between Mila and Jakob fizzled out and a new tension arose—one marked by the trail of Baz's eyes on Mila. It took him less than three seconds to give in—he threw his shoes off making no complaint of the time and darted toward the back patio.

"Race you guys there," he said.

Mila and Jakob both gasped in fake-shock and each ripped off a piece of clothing on their race to the hot tub—Mila kicked off her shoes, slid off her dress, and Jakob became less and less of a Tweed with each chuckle and stumble over clothing being taken off.

Mila liked this. There was no awkwardness in the air, only a playful curiosity and a desire to end the night relaxed. Nothing really mattered to any of them at this point, and she never thought she would get here—face to face with Baz in a hot tub accompanied by someone she had just met.

The sky was soft, the clouds floated with ease, and the stars were not entirely visible—light was still polluting the night, but the moon was now waxing, a perfect crescent following the full moon under which Mila first had the urge to let go.

The conversation amongst the trio was kind and the bubbles in the water were equally as gentle. There was nothing abrasive about the end of this night, as one would imagine situations like this might be. The two men were laughing side by side, talking of meaningless things—but their chatter in between genuine laughs meant something to Mila. It was a sign of her effort to be alive, of company worth forgetting problems with. She loved this ease, she wished she could capture it in a poem or an indie film made just for her own viewing from bed on the laziest of days.

Baz and Jakob were clear opposites, Mila realized, but they both had something of each other within them.

Maybe they were designed as such, so as to appear in front of Mila one day—so she can notice their differences, not to pit them against each other, but to make note of how people carry bits and pieces of one another in themselves without realizing it. We are all other people on the inside, Mila thought. She was amazed by the revelation that everyone is a library of borrowed traits and jokes, vocabularies and mannerisms. She slowly sipped on the thought of finding herself not just in one person, but two—because they both had, too—and suddenly she was intoxicated with the idea, reveling in the beauty of finding meaning in a forewarned desolate world.

"You're being really quiet, Mila," Baz noted.

The two men were relaxed, arms spread out amongst the ledge of the hot tub, their eyes low with the tiredness of spending many hours awake. Mila noticed she was relaxed, too, moving her hands to feel the push and pull of whirling water amongst bodies not her own.

"That's new!" Jakob blurted.

"New? I hardly know you," Mila joked.

"How long have you known each other?" Baz asked.

"A week now," Jakob answered.

"Ah, so you don't know each other at all," Baz said.

"Well, the same could be said about all of us," Jakob said, teasing as if he knew something.

Baz and Mila exchanged a look of questioning, indicating neither of them had told Jakob about their history, if one could call it that at all.

"Yup!" Mila said, "We're all just some new friends," and she felt that it was true.

Baz seemed uneasy with her answer, as if he didn't like the implication of keeping a secret from Jakob. It didn't seem like a big deal to just tell him they knew each other for a while, but knew each other as in *knew of* each other since they'd exchanged conversations, jokes, and the hint of a promised kiss over the years—which led to nothing at all. It was, indeed, not worthy of a secret. This was what Mila thought that Baz thought—she, of course, could have no idea how he perceived the situation.

Baz laughed, "We do know each other actually. We met a few years ago through some friends."

Jakob was in on the secret.

"Oh! Small world, then," Jakob said.

Nothing more was said, so his sentence hung in the air like laundry that refuses to dry.

A small minute later, Mila decided it was time to go back to her bed and unravel the rest of the night there, with her eyes on the sky through her bedroom window. She lifted herself out of the hot tub—her skin glistening with wetness under the moon's glow. She sat at the ledge for a moment, considering what would happen if she stayed longer. But, admittedly, to explore the opportunity would be to ruin whatever progress she'd made, and though she whole-heartedly did want to stay, she knew nothing would ever live up to the romance of leaving a possibility for the future on the table.

Reaching over for a towel, Mila broke the silence everyone was enjoying, "I better get going," she told the men.

Quicker than she let out the last word of her statement, Baz harked back that he must get going, too. Following each other out of the water, the three of them dried off and made their way back into the house. Mila put her dress back on and Baz, his clothes from the drier. Jakob wrapped himself in his bathrobe and wore a tired smile as if the hot tub had evaporated his animations. Mila saw the curve of his lips melt into his face, settling into the tiny crevices by the sides of his lips—she was slowly becoming familiar with his different expressions.

A few short goodbyes later, Baz and Mila found themselves on the street. She considered that seeing her must have made him have a change of heart, too, especially given the haste with which he declared his desire to leave after her.

"Bye," he said, still looking at her.

She stared at him blankly, half expecting more. She gulped down her anticipation of what could happen next, and got over it by ending the night there.

"See you," she said, turning away to walk home.

Mila looked back to check on the effect of her nonchalant exit, and Baz simply looked unaffected. He was walking in the opposite direction, hands in pockets, under the sparse light of the streetlamps offering moments of mystery and clarity all within the same stretch. He looked back at her momentarily, pausing his walk, but said nothing at all; instead, he turned the corner.

She was mesmerized by the empty street—it was electric to have crossed paths again. She imagined she could have run up to him, pushed him in jest—he would've pushed her back, they would have laughed, or fought, or something in between.

But the street was empty, save her and her longing eyes.

V.

A (LITTLE) DEATH

Sundays had this way of making the rest of the week stretch out, only to bookend memory and truth with another day of serene nothing—worship in the truest sense of the word.

If a deity is to be held in the highest of graces, spending the day in passing—in unengaged thoughts or engaging in thoughts not one's own through literature—is what worship ought to be, Mila thought. She thought about the way people made themselves small to appease a god. She thought about the sacrifices people make to fulfil the human desire to connect with something bigger. Her favourite was the eroticism of kneeling, the way people kneel to show love, to propose love, to admit love, to plead and beg, to devour…all of it tasted like god—and lunacy in the best possible sense of the word.

Mila's mind was crawling back to how Baz had left their encounter the week before: he looked like he wanted to say something but remained untouched by the pull of prayers she'd sent out in the past. Admittedly, they had been sent into the universe, and not to him directly, but Mila knew that radiating the energy of desire consequently oozed onto its target, laying out a sticky mess for one to either relish or clean. It is a web of love intended to reel in a feast—love is always glazed with hunger, she thought. At times, she wanted to devour Baz and for him to devour her—the contents of her personality, mind, her way of seeing life. She wanted to be devoured, but this was, of course, a remaining thought of her past ways, before the letter made obvious the wedge between the romance in her mind and the eagerness of reality to move on—despite her pouring out her heart at all costs.

Mila pulled out her journal from the bedside table that rocked upon each impact or graze of the fingers to its knob. Her sheets were warm this morning, and she had surrendered to them, worshiping the holiest place of all—where there is always respite, and rest, and love, and crying, and phone calls, and movies that look like mirrors except one is required to search for the reflection. Films and art are not true mirrors, she thought, rather they are imagined and pondered upon to create meaning.

Her journal was gold embroidered, a design of mystical sorts, stars and moons, and lines in directions that question the shape of fruits. She was looking for a poem written last year in dedication to Baz. There was no particular reason for her sudden obsession with the poem, rather she was intrigued by ideas of her past-self and the way she had held such high regard for him in the intimate space between pages of her innermost thoughts. The poem was more so about her than him, at this point. It would reveal the him she had built up and fed, perpetuating certain ways of being in her mind—the poem was, of course, about her experience *of* him.

Flipping through the pages delicately, each making a gentle sound of gratitude while joining the piled others between covers, Mila remembered writing the poem, how she had been in a frenzy to figure things out. She had been trying to "get over it" for as long as she knew him, but now she really felt like it was happening, she was moving out of the way. Sure, looking at him would still make her feel alive, in the easiest sense of the word, but there was only *some* yearning on her part, her words only dripped of a *bit* of desire, and her eyes only revealed a *tiny* inkling of rhythms only familiar to her in the little dark of night, wax-sealed between drifting and dreaming.

Only Alive on Sundays

Mila landed on the poem. She knew it held sentiment to her past-self, and she wanted to honour the version of her that awoke feeling bruised every morning—for there was someone she wanted that did not want her back. It felt like she was having her intestines wrung out every time rejection faced her, whether from him or not. It was all a reminder of existing in a world while being too much or not enough. She moved the string bookmark sitting placidly on the page, and read her poem aloud:

> *I am not interested in your star sign*
> *to know if you are my type of human.*
> *I want to know what you say about the*
> *stars, to learn about the energies that collided*
> *when you came to be, to understand*
> *the patterns of the cosmos, to know*
> *which transits give rise to something holy.*
> *I am only interested in worship*
> *when it is in front of you.*

A gasp escaped her mouth as an audible end to the poem—Mila was surprised at both the honesty and the deception in the poem. The erotic had always been the culprit of blurred lines between sinning and saving, but at the time that she had written the poem, she was worshipping and being worshipped by someone else, and to imagine her mind elsewhere, in prayer of Baz, made her feel guilty. It was as if being in love with him never really gave her the opportunity to be present. She knew her mind-TV was on for so long that, at some point, she forgot to exist outside of the scene. She was one to imagine her life in stills—poetic captions and portrayals of the romantic to induce a sort of desire that paints reality green, but whether it be through love or envy was unbeknownst to her. She knew this to be the colour of both feelings because each sprouted from a place of desire—green from the heart depicts love, a brighter hue of the colour to show desire in the purest form, in appreciation of it. Green from the eyes denotes envy—a murkier version of the colour—it highlights the desire of something not had, the recognition of its wanting, the understanding that this version of reality is marked by its lack.

Mila considered her motivations with Baz—revealing the truth to herself would be the entirety of how she could fully get over it. Her intentions were pure at times, when she really felt seen, but she mostly wanted to be acquainted with him so deeply that they merged into the same person. Maybe she wanted to cease existing as herself by being devoured by him. With her mind-TV taking a break as she had gained more clarity, it was easier now to see how she was barely living—and what a privilege it was to be devoid of meaning outside of someone else giving it to her! She knew she had to fill her mind with ways to actually *be* herself now.

While lying in stillness, figuring out the chaos of being alive, the doorbell beckoned Mila to the barrier of within and without. Putting on her robe, Mila positioned her eye to the peephole as if to a camera trying to get the best shot. She saw Jakob, more dishevelled than usual, looking back and forth between his watch and the door. Mila felt his urgency and swung open the door, tucking her hair away neatly.

"Everything alright?" she asked.

"I didn't have your number so I couldn't call you, but I was passing by Luna on my way to grab some coffee and heard a cacophony of clanking coming from the window. I think—"

Mila interrupted him.

"Thanks for letting me know! I'll deal with it today," she said, quickly yet easily.

Jakob looked confused, a little bewildered, and maybe impressed with the calmness with which she was reacting. The truth was that she was annoyed. Lunacy at Luna was the last thing she wanted to deal with on a Sunday, especially when she was just about to begin her worship of the old poets.

"Alright. No problem, I'll check back in later?"

"Sure," she said, "Come to the shop in a couple of hours if you're free."

He nodded and turned to leave before Mila beckoned him back with a question.

"Wait, how did you know where I lived?" Mila asked.

"Oh, well I had Baz's number, and since you guys are already acquainted, I thought I might ask him if he knew your address, and he did."

Mila was surprised that Baz remembered where she lived since he had never actually entered her home—he did, conveniently, know of the park just across the street when she had told him to meet her there once. But he never did meet her there. How Jakob found her unit was beyond Mila, but knowing him, he likely knocked on every door to find her and inform her of the emergency.

"Okay, see you later," she told him, rushing to close the door and change.

Mila made her way to Luna with a pep named haste in her step. She tried to breathe, relax—she knew that if she were to make a commotion, the shop would engage in more chaos. This was one of the instances in which she understood nothing about Luna. If she was ever in the mood to rip reality apart, the portal section reflected that. At the moment she turned the corner, she expected there to be letters and poems ripped up, tornadoing in the shop, leaves somehow rustling themselves and making a disastrous scene. Perhaps there would be leakage of some sort. Mila knew getting over Baz actually meant killing off a part of herself, but she did not dare to imagine Luna be involved.

The key in the lock rattled her body before opening the door, and there was nothing to witness but the calm after the storm. Mila entered slowly, locking the door behind her. The shop was messy, but no carnage had taken place. No leaks, no paper floating in the air. Instead—on the ground—there were heaps of masks in, somewhat, neat piles. Most were colourful, some black with lace—those reminded her of a masquerade ball—others were more odd, settling into the depths of the uncanny valley. They bore her own face with slight alterations—it seemed as if Mila's face had been peeled and marked with a mole or a crook of the nose. There laid versions of herself in alternate possibilities, she guessed. With her stomach clenched as if to hold on to all the air in her lungs—for if her breaths were to escape she might fall into the abyss—she sat at the windowsill at the front of the shop considering the piles, unsure of the meaning behind the mess.

She decided to sit with the masks. As creepy as it was for her to approach her own face amongst other more ballroom-style masks, Mila needed to understand them, to ask them their story, perhaps find out, or make out, their meaning. She picked out the most seductive one—poutier lips doused in red, eyes made more doe-like, and an expression of modern evils held within its eyes. She let it rest in her hands with her own eyes closed for a while—it felt almost alive, beating and squirming in her hand, palpitations reverberating through the delicate bones in her fingers. Though in appearance, it looked to remain distant and without movement. After moments of near-quiet contemplation, the air had grown so still as if to suffocate the life out of both her and the masks. She let out a deep breath.

Finally, Mila's instinct drew her hands upward, and she placed the mask on her face.

VI.

THE WORLD (IS MINE OYSTER)[4]

Mila laid the mask flat against her face, smoothing down the sides for the two faces to become one. Her own face was perhaps a mask on any other day, but, today, it remained the most authentic thing about her—it had not been changed, unless someone was to count the change of circling the sun for twenty-seven and a half years. Or, 1424 Sundays. The squishing of flesh on flesh made a noise not unfamiliar to those who have kneaded dough on an oiled surface, stirred a pot of macaroni, or listened to the sound of themselves chewing gum. Having a layer of someone else glued to her face sent a chill down Mila's spine—each vertebra quaked into the next finally settling into a united posture of complete discomfort.

    She grabbed the edge of the cushion she was sitting on, feeling as though it might magic-carpet her away into some dream or hazy vision. But alas, no such whimsical event took place. Her attention was on the skin of her face—she could feel the sliming of metaphorical worms between her own face and the other. The two were perhaps fusing—each nerve ending meeting to jolt the face into action, she imagined. She wanted to peel the mask off and escape the horror of her freshly acquired countenance. Though, she knew that would not please whatever entity had manifested the masks in the first place. A lesson was upon her, and as annoying as it was to be forced to learn something out of a situation she desperately just wanted to feel through, Mila acquainted herself with one of the antique mirrors on the least excitable shelf in the shop.

Stabilizing reality with a touch to her face, Mila witnessed her mirrored reflection—it was an act of betrayal: her normal reflection of self was now a distorted projection similar to those typically found in a funhouse. Mila noticed the comparison to be an exaggeration, for the face was pretty, and not at all *distorted*, but it made her queasy to be herself, just not quite.

As if experiencing the world for the first time, she found her fine motor skills not so fine after all. Each movement of an index finger expected to lay upon the tip of her nose reached the bridge instead. Disoriented, Mila took a long look at this potential of herself. She wondered if this version existed elsewhere—else*time*—and was missing her face on a random afternoon, screaming that there must be something wrong. She imagined that this version of her, perhaps named Lila, was still asleep in an apartment that looked somewhat like hers—maybe the layout was merely mirrored and the bathroom tiles, a pinker tone reserved for sunset peaking through clouds in mid-August. As she refined the details of Lila's reality, the architecture of the slightly altered timeline began taking shape under Mila's feet.

The mind-TV had been turned on, but Mila was viewing *from* the inside: the lens—Lila's eyes—and her perspective—one of being dollied around. Mila could feel the sensations of Lila's arm grazing a sheet, goosebumps raising in shock to the sensitivity born out of a new day, her senses being rebooted, ready to process the data that is being alive.

Familiar in her own bed, Mila could see a shoulder just beyond her fingertips' reach, but she was not in control of the body she was presently inhabiting. It felt as though mind and body were missing a connective layer of communication. She could hear every one of Lila's thoughts, despite not being the one to *have* the thoughts. Mila was now a witness to the happenings of Lila's life.

Only Alive on Sundays

It occurred to Mila that she may be in a crisis of sorts, and perhaps she was, but this was not to the extreme of madness that one might imagine. It was not a spiral, rather, a revelation. Those lines are, admittedly, commonly blurred, but she felt safe enough in Lila's reality to not fully panic. She knew Jakob and Baz likely existed in this reality, almost indistinguishable from her own versions of them, and though they had only recently started a friendship, she sensed that if needed, they would help her.

Lila rolled over, grasping the body beside her, and the front-row view excited Mila—her mouth was gaping on the inside in anticipation of finding out who it would be. She saw a bare-chested man exposing a grin familiar to Mila as Jakob's. The ease of a Sunday settled in at his sight. Lila ran a thumb down his cheek and Mila felt it in her bones—the affection between the two rippled through Mila's heart and, once again, she saw her vulnerable heart beating in her chest, echoing with simplicity. The two characters exchanged morning niceties and Mila felt herself rise with the swift motions of Lila's legs swinging out to the side of the bed—opposite to the one which Mila enjoys. Lila placed her feet into fuzzy slippers, their softness massaged Mila's soles, and a feather tickled her right pinky with its delicate grazing. Mila inwardly sighed out a relief.

Lila kindly told the Jakob-like man that she is to make some coffee, sweet just how he likes it. She grabbed a book and escorted herself past the door frame marked with dates which were missing the height indications that typically accompany such data. This was a new scene for Mila.

Lila ripped the journal open with haste at the kitchen island while checking back on the bedroom with her eyes. Consequently, Mila only got a glance of the fingerprints in the notebook—all stained red, and smelling slightly of rust. To the untrained eye, it may have seemed like an art project of sorts, but Mila recognized the blood-inked journal from Luna. A few months had passed, but it was unshakeable—that journal did not belong to Mila, yet it had found its way to the portal section one day when she was in search of an old amulet. Bearing similarity to Mila's own journal, she had fingered through the pages looking for a sign, perhaps from the future of what was to come, or where the necklace may be. But she had only found pictures of men with names underneath and a confirmation of if "it" had worked, or not.

Lila took out a marker and began writing under the entry for her Jakob:

> *It worked! All I had to do was alter the recipe for the morning brew! Two teaspoons of blood drawn from my left ring finger instead of one. Add honey for sweetness.*

Feeling her own stomach turn, Mila reached down to offer warmth to the sensitive disgust growing inside her. With a hurl forward, as if to release the toxins growing within her through an eager open mouth, she was back at Luna. She shucked the mask off—it oozed a goopy liquid homogenous with saliva—and threw it straight into the trash in the corner. Its eyes stared back at her, the face seemingly pulsating with life in the folds of the black bag lining the container. Mila felt her transience coming to an end; finding her footing back in the shop, she looked in the mirror again, making sure her face was just as she remembered. An odd way for a lesson to be learned, she thought, despite not understanding the lesson at all. The evil she had sensed in Lila's eyes was perhaps a conjuring that smelled more of desperation than ill-intent. Though feeding unknowing men your blood is horrific, in the most applicable sense of the word, was it not adjacent to putting out an air of utmost desire where it is certainly not wanted? It reeked of the same desperation, she realized.

Mila stepped away from the garbage, imagining it screeching, despite the stillness that overtook the shop. She flattened down her shirt and closed her eyes to ground herself and breathe in the present. She saw Baz in a dark void—if she reached out, he would back away more distance than was necessary. She felt small, belittled, in comparison. Mila fell witness to the realization that the soft-spot which she held for Baz was making him all the more unreachable. He got pushed away or up into a fleeting angelic state—and she, pushed away or down into the depths of earth or maybe even beyond it to a personal hell disguised as a lusty plane of hedonism. It was not a magnetically attractive soft-spot, rather, it was a repulsive one—in the most scientific sense of the word. She knew this fact a million times over, so it was not a sudden realization, rather a deepening of something she had uncovered through her own insistence to get over it. Mila further owed some acknowledgement of the heavy work to Jakob—he had recently shown her friendship, and it was thirst-quenching for Mila to form a bond with him—him who was a fresh slate that also mirrored Baz so fluently.

Picking up the masks, both the ones alike to her and not, Mila noticed another version of herself—deeply happy in the eyes, crow's feet formed by years of smiling and laughter. The shape of her features remained the same, almond eyes painted brown by swirls of honey dribble and this version even had a cheekier, more grand smile. Mila wanted to try it on for size—to taste the happiness reflected in this face—but she decided not to. She told herself that she did not want to experience any other version of herself. She considered Lila's backstory and what brought her to a place of such debauchery. Mila nearly wanted to applaud her on her craft, but she knew that she could never fully understand her not having lived Lila's life through and through. She could only understand herself, if that, and the experiences she had, which were perhaps not so different than anyone else's.

The smallness that takes up so much space in Mila's mind is likely there for others, too, in varied palpitations—felt in locked away hearts ripe with bloodlust every time a reality is confirmed or denied. And Mila had just learned she would never be able to change anything about herself if she could not accept the experiences that had brought her to this very point in life. Becoming who she wants to be is magical yet violent, Mila thought, for she must be willing to kill the part of her that begs to remain within the familiar walls of everyday thoughts. Removing the stain of habit—be it love or hate—would require her to strip off the layers of stories she'd made up and believed.

Placing the remaining masks on top of the suffocating mass of Lila, Mila tied up the bag and unlocked the door to take the chaos out to the larger deposit of unwanted goods behind the shop.

At the garbage bins, Mila rearranged a few items to ensure the bag's secrecy. Turning to get away from Luna's vicinity, something caught her eye—Mila noticed Jakob's grandfather's painting. The canvas was aching for its last breath—ripped open through the middle—trickling with droplets of sun-gold and forming a curious puddle just beneath its frame.

VII.

THE DEVIL
(IS IN THE DETAILS)

Mila spotted Jakob walking toward the shop out of the corner of her eyes. It was early evening—the sky was almost ready to take a break from light—and Mila felt slightly jet-lagged; her trip took more time than she thought it would have. She took him in from a distance, finding gratitude for his insistence on checking up on her. He wasn't in his usual tweed, though was still very much emanating Tweed traits. Rather, he had light-washed jeans on, buckled at the hip with a black leather belt, and a grey t-shirt. The most basic of outfits, yet unbecomingly attractive on him. It looked more like something Baz would wear, and perhaps he had been rubbing off on Jakob—each of them had likely showed the other the ropes of their idea of manhood just by existing.

Mila approached Jakob who was peering into the shop with a hand cupped above his eye to block out the glare on the window. He was trying the doorknob for the second time, it seemed, when she broke the silence.

"Hi," she said, maybe shyly, maybe drained from being Lila.

"Looks like everything sorted itself out,' he said, "What happened earlier?"

"Some portal drama. Nothing to get your research glasses on for," she responded, feeling immediately rejuvenated by teasing him.

"I happen to like seeing," he said.

"Great! Mind telling me why I *saw* your grandfather's painting in the trash then?" she said, with a tone of mock excitement, "And *what* are you wearing?"

"Two great questions, Mila. Care to join me inside and I'll indulge you on the day's secrets?" he suggested, sly of voice.

"Honestly, I don't feel like being in there after all the clean-up. Can we go somewhere else?"

"My place? Hot tub may or may not be on the table."

And that, she could resist, but did not want to.

They walked the distance to Jakob's with him filling her in on his dress of choice: Jakob was to meet an ex, who notably despised his Tweed exterior, and so he thought he would play it down a little. But upon clothing himself in an outfit he'd never think of wearing, with Baz's help, of course, he had questioned whether he needed to meet her at all if he had to go to such lengths to appear appealing. So, he had called off the meeting and showed up at Luna to see if all was right on Mila's end of life. Mila could empathize with Jakob—she too had changed herself from time to time just to impress Baz in one of the potential cameos she so deeply wished to make in his life.

"I'm glad you came," she told Jakob, genuinely, heartfelt, maybe sadly.

"And about the painting," Jakob said slowly, almost afraid to broach the subject, "Well, first, thank you. I wouldn't have had it without you. But, that thing is incredibly annoying. Every night since I've had it, I've slept horribly."

Mila raised an eyebrow at that, "So that's why you wanted us to stay that night after your party!" she said, as if catching him in some act.

"Yeah...the house feels oddly lonesome when it's just me and that shining thing. You and Baz really eased my nocturnal tendencies that night."

"Right, so the gash?" Mila asked.

"Right. The gash. This is harder for me to admit than I'd like, but I think that painting was bringing out the worst in me somehow. Perhaps the fact is due to its obnoxious light, and therefore my lack of sleep...which would lead to some undeserved crankiness."

He paused between his previous and next thought, emphasizing the encounter's surrealism.

"Basically, it was having some kind of *Dorian Gray* effect on me."

"Right, so the gash?" Mila asked again, this time with more of a jokey air.

"I threw my alarm clock at it," he said, "They were both getting on my last nerve."

A devious laugh escaped Mila's lungs at the idea of Jakob waking up and throwing his alarm clock at the painting.

The sun was nearly setting and they were almost at their destination. Mila felt relieved to laugh, to not have to be so serious, despite how serious Jakob could seem at times. He always had a lightness to him that she wasn't particularly jealous of, but it was tinged with a green she could not easily categorize as either love or envy. Perhaps it was both. She looked at the now golden sun laying on his face while he unlocked his front door. She glanced at his hands fidgeting with the keys and the doorknob—this obstacle before entry was a tease of sorts, brimming with the anticipation of the door miraculously unlocking for the two of them.

"You just have to jiggle it a little," he let her know.

"Jiggle it," she repeated, nodding.

The interaction made Mila feel as though she had known Jakob for years. She felt that she could easily trace the crevices of his life and know him deeply simply because he would allow her to. Because he wasn't going to hold back on words, or feelings, or temptations. She assumed she could let herself in.

Passing through the threshold once again, Mila took her shoes off on the Persian rug decorating the entrance of Jakob's home. Its red hues marked with gold embroidery were warm and inviting, and the small details of flowers indicated a foreign sweetness. Perhaps Mila was reading into it a bit much, observing the rug so delicately as to avoid eye contact with Jakob. She did not want to look up, to find him looking at her, to be wrought with emotions—since she now found herself tip-toeing toward a fine line. He caught her eye as he was kneeling to untie his sneakers, new and un-scuffed. They held their look for a moment longer—not felt as an eternity, but as the opening of a new chapter. And as if channeling Baz, or perhaps recalling a joke between the three of them, "Race you there?" he propositioned.

She was not caught off guard by the sentiment, for she expected it to be him who broke the silence. Replaying the scene from the party, save their third party, they took off into the backyard once again, shedding layers to make space for the discomfort of night's cold embrace. They plunged into the water—Jakob switched on the jets and Mila settled into a corner with the comfiest ledge to sit on. She was enjoying the silence of shared company in its most serene form—with her eyes closed—when Jakob flicked the tiniest droplet of water on her face.

Being reminded of the mask taking shape on her face, Mila overreacted with a jolt and vigorous rubbing of her cheek. Realizing she wasn't alone, she peeled open an eye only to be met with Jakob's inquisitive face.

Mila found herself not wanting to share all the details with Jakob given his involvement, but she started speaking anyway.

"At Luna. There was this thing, with some masks, and I don't want to get into it, but it was traumatic."

"Masks?"

He was about to inquire further, but he must have noticed how unsettled she looked. Instead, he offered to go get her a drink—as if that would be the solution.

She meant to tell him it's all alright, that it was for the better, that she needed the wake-up call. But that felt too hard, and she was relaxed in the water, so instead she asked him for a joint and punctuated the question with a sweet smile, assuming the answer to be "surely not," as Jakob likely did not partake in such things.

And to Mila's surprise, he answered in the affirmative and turned to man-handle a wooden box nearby. He teased Mila first by holding a pre-roll up to her mouth, but as she reached in for it, he quickly switched the direction around and placed it delicately in between his own lips. Laughter spewed out of Mila which made Jakob's face grow mischievous with a small smile.

"You thought it was just for you?" Jakob asked her teasingly.

"No, of course it's to share! Let's share. I need to see you let your Tweed down," she told him excitedly.

In an instant she regretted saying that as he might find offense in the sentiment, but his smile only expanded wider letting her know that his Tweed was *already* down— that they were near-strangers in a hot tub partially naked, anyway. How much more un-Tweed-like could he get?

Mila felt herself ease into the water more after each exhale, and though the joint at hand was not the type she was used to, she was relaxed; the incident from earlier in the day was already escaping her mind.

Wading her arms in the water, witnessing its movement just as she had done last week, her hand bumped Jakob's and she could not say much more than *oh*, because she was not sorry at all and she could only notice the happy accident. His hands had been on her mind since she had watched him unlock the door, but it felt strange to say nothing at all, so she followed the previous word with "sorry."

"Don't be sorry," he said, grabbing her hand and pulling her closer to himself.

She let the now still water carry her toward him. Mila settled into his lap, each leg finding a delicate balance on the outside of his. Jakob carried the hand he was still holding onto and placed it on his chest. She followed his lead and did the same with her other hand. The moment was intoxicating and she did not want to do anything but revel in it for the approaching few Sundays. She felt his hands on her back—soft from being submerged in water—and she wanted him to pull her even closer, to fill the gap of whatever friendship remained between them. She wanted to plant her lips on his to "get over it."

She took her time to consider if she should follow through with her desires. Although he was not Baz, and not particularly the man of concern, she wondered whether it would aid or abet her to partake in The Tweed.

"It's night," she said, "I should go sleep."

"What does night have to do with sleep?" he replied.

She smiled, catching him in a proposition he likely did not know she would understand.

"Night has better sweets to prove,[5]" she replied while raising an eyebrow.

Jakob's eyes grew wide as he seemingly was not expecting Mila to understand the implication of his very Tweed quoting of Milton. The subtle flirtation made it all the more unclear who the forbidden fruit was between the two of them.

Jakob kept his eyes on her steadily as she considered her options. He offered her patience while still maintaining a firm grip on her back. He sensed the mood turn darker and likely read it to be seductive, but on Mila's end, it was her slow approach on vengeance settling in. Vengeance in the sense that she had let so many years pass while completely missing out on the rest of the world simply because Baz existed. She wanted to avenge the version of herself that felt like she had to sit out a round.

She pressed her lips to his, feeding off the energy he kindly, softly returned. She squeezed her legs tighter together, making Jakob more aware of her body under the water. Again, she wanted the scene to go on longer than she had lived. To live in its beauty would be a glorious feat, and she was not only responsible for it, but enjoying it, too. He kissed her neck, inhaling the scent of nectarines and salt on her body. They created a space somewhere between the world and the belly of the underworld. Desire and anticipation have a way of making us feel as though we are not in or of the world, Mila thought, but rather escaping it momentarily to carve out an energy field just for the people involved—to take in the scent of another's body, to taste the rawness of the universe within someone else. People sink into the underworld so as to raise above it in haste, deliberately marking the delectable end of making magic. Magic is due, she realized.

Mila rocked in his lap and Jakob took the cue to inch his fingers higher on her back to unclasp the unholy garment standing between them.

"Wait," she said instinctively, speaking lowly, "Baz—"

Realizing the sin she had just committed, she pulled back and opened her eyes.

Evidently, she was not "over it."

VIII.

THE MAGICIAN
(NEVER REVEALS HIS SECRETS)

Mila was in recovery the next Sunday. She was love-drunk and the whole universe—or what people know of it—knew. She nursed a hangover credited only to late nights and stolen moments between *hello*s and *goodbye*s—this was her one day of self-reverence and solitude. Most days, she found meaning in opening the shop—sweeping up, making the place an altar of sorts to the guardians of time—but with each passing Sunday, she had begun to dread it. Her soul was not there on Sundays. Rather, it was off making dinner plans with the past and future—not to escape the day, but to fall into it more deeply, to understand the potential of existing non-linearly.

*

It had only been a week since her slip-up, and although days passed smoothly after, she had not known in the moment if she would live it down or if Jakob would be mad or flattered or sad or vengeful, though none of those things were outwardly Jakob-like. They had taken a breather—he had gently pushed her aside and they had sat beside each other, the outside of their thighs still grazing the skin of the other underwater. The silence that had flowed between them seemed like a communication that could only be read by a psychic. It had been full of friction, of *what's he thinking?* or an assumed *do I look like Baz?*

Jakob had finally broken the thickness between them.

"Did you just call me Baz?" he had asked.

All she *could* do was own up to it. It was true her interests still laid in the palm of Baz's hand, but she had

Only Alive on Sundays

been so distraught, yet intrigued, by the experience of Lila and her Jakob. Perhaps Mila had needed a taste of that reality to see what this one could look like when accompanied by Jakob—out of his own volition.

"I did. Sorry. But," she had said slowly, "only because I was thinking about how close the two of you have gotten recently," she'd admitted.

And that was only partially true. The full truth would have been to say that her lips were trained in both mouthing and trying to forget Baz's name, and not yet Jakob's—but that would have been too much for Jakob to digest, she assumed.

"While you were kissing me?" he had remarked, inquisitively.

"I mean you were dressed like him today, can you really blame me?"

"I guess not," he had said, firmly—though he still seemed to be considering if he could blame her or not.

He had looked to have forgiven her, but they did not continued on. Instead, they had remained seated next to each other, talking of this or that, and the night was somehow made more poetic. They had shared a night's ease before he had walked her home. The pause in their rendezvous was seemingly a character in their story playing the part of self-control. Mila had learned then that she had more work to do before she could enter into something non-Baz related, and so she was grateful to Baz for his interruption.

She had seen the pattern just then—he appeared in her life every time she was making a big change, getting ready to move on from what never actually was—except, maybe, a tacit agreement of their shared pleasure in looking at each other. She thought to call it sabotage and, perhaps, he would call it magic on his end. <u>For was it not a spell, or a curse in someone else's dictionary, to always be on someone's mind?</u> Mila had wondered how he managed that—what sort of energy was *he* putting out? Was he not also laying a sticky web for *her* to fall into head-first?

Despite her incessant demand to get *over* it before getting *into* it, the week had passed with Mila and Jakob enjoying sunsets, the quirks of Luna, and each other when the time was right.

*

Mila lazily fluffed out her white comforter while still in bed. The motion disturbed the air in the room sending wind in all directions. She laid in bed for minutes longer, sinking into the comfort of Sunday, of having someone want to spend time with her, of the nectarine pit on her bedside table sitting in the stillness of having been consumed, a dried layer of its sweetness still glazing the crevices of the seedling. She examined it for a few moments longer and caught the sunlight offering a hazy sheen to one side of the fruit, while the other was subdued in shadow.

A message dinged on her phone, and simultaneously, she heard a letter slip into her apartment— the shuffling noise of paper sent a pleasant, yet nervous, tingle down to her stomach. Feeling as though she had swallowed a fruit whole—seed and all—she did not know which message to address first. It could be any letter, but it could also be from the ether.

She then decided, once and for all, that she would take Sundays for herself. Mila found that her boundaries were respected by the universe, as she was telling it she no longer cared to be notified of every little energetic goings-on. Mila began wondering if the Three Swords Bookshop down the street from Luna was open on Sundays and made a mental note to check later. For now, she would check her phone, the letter could wait for a business day. A text from Jakob awaited her: *Meet me at the market?*

Although she intended to be in solitude for the day—re-setting her energy, filling her space with music, transmuting whatever ache was still in her into a feeling of utmost bliss—she reminded herself that all of that could still happen after going to the market. She had to get produce, anyway, and seeing Jakob momentarily would be no inconvenience. She imagined him striding along the stalls of the market, catching her glance, enveloping her in blue butterflies, making her all the more dizzy just with a smile. She thought he looked especially enchanting with his beard grown out—he, being too busy with Mila and careless enough, was perhaps also filled with the intoxicating sense of love typically afforded to the first week of a blossoming relationship. He always appeared so sturdy, despite his own vices. Mila's excitement to see him at the market launched her out of bed quicker than she could text him back that she'd see him there.

She spritzed herself in a summery perfume laced with magnolia flowers and ripe nectarines, buckled her overalls over a white turtleneck, and grabbed the mesh bag intended for fruits and vegetables off the hook by the door. The sun was hitting its usual spot, nearly highlighting the letter on the ground, calling to her attention not only its presence but its blankness. It elevated her a little to know someone was thinking of her, and being so consumed by Jakob the past week, she settled on him as the sorcerer of the letter.

Approaching the square, Mila noticed the colour of the leaves had changed to a deeper red and orange, some a more subtle, darker, green. It felt as though seasons had switched and she had failed to fall witness to the cooler temperature, despite her reaching for warmer clothes out of instinct. She considered that her body always knew, from the inside, exactly what to anticipate, how to prepare her for the reception of weather, and touch, and feelings, and events, and water—hot or cold.

She found him with her eyes—Jakob stood at some stall or another enjoying a plum or another adjacent fruit. He bit into it with a slow thrust, his lips parting to catch the initial juice that fruits spew out of their broken skin. She considered how delicate men are when eating fruit. She thought she truly knew him at that moment as he was sorting nectarines with one hand into a small produce bag. Mila liked how he maintained his Tweed tendencies *despite* the activity he was participating in. Despite, despite, despite. She was happy he had chosen to see her through, despite her calling him another name. To him, it was any name, so it did not sting as much as it should have. Regardless of the harrowing fear of Jakob letting Baz in on the slip-up, she was incredibly in awe. Mila thought she could watch Jakob from a distance for two and a half eternities, perhaps a thousand Sundays over, but she knew better than to fall into the trap of yearning.

Jakob noticed her walking toward him and pointed to his own white long-sleeve. She looked at his top first, then slowly down at her own, exaggerating the comparison happening in real-time for him.

She planted a childish kiss on his cheek and said, "Except mine doesn't have a stain on the front."

He looked down to the deep red speckle on his shirt—it gave the impression of memory caught in a quilt. He laughed, his lips stained a deeper shade from the fruit, as well.

"Yet," he replied, with a smile and a knowing nod.

Baz was no longer what she wanted. She decided so just then.

And, as if to contradict her, to test her one last time, Baz was across the stall, looking at them, looking—in amazement—at Mila under Jakob's arm.

"Big fan of nectarines?" Baz teased Jakob, eyeing his overflowing bag.

"Sipping them, especially," Jakob responded, his voice marked with an indistinguishable hint of innuendo.

Both Baz and Mila burst out laughing—she stole a look from Baz and he one from her. Jakob seemed to grow shy as he likely meant it as a small joke, and their intense reactions did not match the quality of the joke. Mila could feel Baz's eyes on her, and she now considered that the blank letter could imply that *he* was thinking of her. They let the laughter die down naturally.

She turned her attention to the vegetables, gathering what she needed for the week ahead while making small talk with the men who now bore more resemblance to one another. She listened to them talk of this and that, just as she and Jakob had done—the men found their own groove in conversation remaining unburdened with Mila's presence.

They were speaking of Jakob's return to teaching the next week, how he'd fallen behind in preparation, when Baz picked up a plum to devour. He perhaps took a hint from Jakob's shirt—the craving to bite into whatever had stained Jakob so happy. Mila took in this repeated sight of a fruit devoured by lips—which she had thought about on countless nights past—as a sign to go home, to enjoy her solitude.

The exchange of goodbyes bled into her walk home—she was lost in time and her journey stretched longer than she knew ten minutes to be, as was typical when enjoying a simple, yet, wanderlust-inducing few moments with one's own appreciation of life.

She put the key to her door and it unlocked with a click. Mila nudged it open. There was a resistance she had never felt there before. Her ears started warming up like bubbles in a pot of boiling water: slowly and with a final burst to the surface in explosive heat. A faint, consistent ringing settled in as she eventually got the door open. And there it was—a pile of blank letters disclosing nothing except an inkling that she was thought of, or worse, spoken about.

IX.

TEMPERANCE

Mila knew exactly what it meant to have the letters at her door poised atop one another—they spoke in unison or, perhaps, as a chorus of shrill reminders. Her assumption was that Baz and Jakob had meandered into the topic of her being. At first thought, the implication of their attention on her knotted her stomach with ecstasy, for had she not wanted this all along? To be the topic of interest amongst Baz and whoever else? In the excitement of the possibility, she felt the air around her stiffen. She stooped low to the ground as she caught herself jumping to conclusions she did not *truly* care for.

In recent days, she had been deliberately vocal about how much she no longer desired Baz, but she also found confirmation of the opposite—it was foreign for her to want someone other than Baz.

Despite how much she wanted to, Mila knew nothing of the nature of the letters—they had potential to be from the men, their conversation dragging on, Jakob filling in details for Baz and his mind to grasp onto, laying out web after web. But they had potential to contradict her too—maybe Baz had filled Jakob in on Mila and the things she'd said she'd do for him—if only he'd allow. Or perhaps neither of those events had transpired. Perhaps Luna was holding a grudge and in some way begging her to open up the shop on Sundays again.

Considering that she could not fathom the inner workings of the universe or the letters, Mila settled for being okay. She found a disturbing comfort in the not knowing. It diminished the eagerness inside her which had

Only Alive on Sundays

gnawed at her mind and heart for an answer that would make everything make sense.

The sun was still speckling the room like a filtered scene intended to wax nostalgic of days spent lazing about—it was as if scented with fresh flowers and caffeine, maybe a poem could be read aloud to invoke the spirit of the poet. They could come to life through their own words, reciting their magic in a way only known to themselves.

Mila took a deep breath sitting at her front door with eyes glued to the letters. Organizing the blank pages as to unburden herself of them through the recycling chute, she recognized a pattern. It unfolded in front of her like a grid finally being exposed—the Y axis and the X axis explaining where their mutual pain fell. She wondered why things were appearing in piles—the masks, the letters. What was it about excess that was seemingly, magically, jamming itself into her life? Were it not for their extremes, would she have taken them seriously? Admittedly, Mila had a tendency to brush off the perceived importance of things. Repeated exposure was how she gained knowledge of truth. She eyed each paper, considering how one would mean nothing at all, but when in company of fifty more, the silent message was so loud that it was just a heart palpitation away from an existential spiral.

Her feelings toward life were always hungry—consumption was on her mind daily and, now, she had figured out that Baz was a feast and her gluttony only became all the more insatiable with each of his withdrawals from her. It is his absence that makes him who he is to her, not his presence. For when he is present, her thoughts veer toward her inability to have, or keep, him—and not toward the ecstasy of being around someone she loves.

Mila cleared the letters—the answer she had so desperately been in search of—from the floor. She left her door open, the sunlight leaking out into the muggy hallway as she walked over to the door dedicated to recycling as to relieve herself from the incessant dribble of the universe.

She liked knowing, understanding, herself deeply. She felt as if she was someone else she was meeting, perhaps merging with, to become herself. To say knowing and acting are the same would not be convincing—knowing she loves to hurt for the sake of love in Baz's name is not the same as putting an end to it, or getting "over it" as the ether had so intrusively commanded her to.

With an added sense of lightness—notably not a removal of heaviness—Mila dumped out the remainder of the letters and walked back into the inviting light of her home. Turning the corner in the hall, a shape took form and she knew it just as one would intimately know where their arm is when awaking from a well-rested night. He was peering into her home in search of her. His back left an impression in the door frame against the light pouring out around him—highlighting *him* against *home*.

"Baz?" she called out to him.

He turned slowly, mumbling a *hi*.

"Can I come in?"

"Sure," she said.

They both scurried in—Baz taking off his shoes smoothly and Mila slipping off her sandals. Mila found herself momentarily excited by the idea of Baz in her home, but then it pained her that she still felt this way. She wondered if he'd come here out of jealousy, which again thrilled her, until she noticed how destabilizing Baz was for her. It was a stark contrast to how rooted she felt with Jakob. Baz's attention always pin-balled her into exorbitant extremes.

"I don't want you to get hurt," he said out of nowhere as she was still settling into the kitchen to make some coffee.

"Why would I get hurt?" she asked carefully as if thinking of each word just before she said it.

Only Alive on Sundays

"I know you're going out with Jakob, and that's fine and all, but when I was helping him pick out some clothes to meet his ex...he just," he paused to think the next part through, "he had a lot to say about her."

His eyebrows shot up as if to say sorry as he looked at her for a response.

"How bad?" Mila asked.

"Not that bad, but I just wouldn't want to hear him talk about you like that. Since we're friends now."

"'We' me and you, or 'we' you and him?"

After a long pause he finally confirmed, "Both."

He looked timid now: his head bowed down, hands in the pocket of his jeans just as he'd placed them after leaving Jakob's party. His shirt was now wearing a similar stain to Jakob's. Perhaps a more yellow fruit had found its way to him after her departure. He looked like Jakob, too—his beard was grown out as if he, too, was distracted by the week's enduring days straining out the last of summer. She noticed it all.

She didn't know if she should be mad at him or full of awe at his, what seemed like, genuine care.

"I like him," Mila said.

I know, he said, with something other than words—more with a look of agony and happiness at the same time. She wanted to melt into him right there—the gluttonous temptation felt more like a once-in-a-life-time delicacy.

"What if..." he started but never finished.

"*What if* what?" she asked, bluntly.

"I never know with you," he said, conceding that it's the knowing on his part and not hers that remains uncertain.

She wanted to close the gap between them but knew that if she did, he would lean into it this time and she would have to tell Jakob. He almost read her mind, deciding to close the gap himself. He held her in her kitchen for a moment, his hands at her waist and hers instinctively at his neck. They stared at each other, her appetite growing, the lust in her eyes finding new fire. She closed her eyes and he, his. A moment of cryptic agreement seeped into their bones. It was not a passionate hug in any sense of the word—rather, it was a loose gripping onto what could be, leaving just enough room for doubt and questions to linger in-between them. They both let go—silently—and he left without saying anything. But it did not feel like a betrayal to Mila, nor forbidden fruit; it was bittersweet like a goodbye left unsaid which oddly left enough room for a *see you again*. Though, she recognized this, too, as her grip on him.

Her Sunday was not unraveling as she'd hoped. Perhaps this was better than any Sunday—spontaneous knowledge found her but, still, the air was not filled with the love she had imagined for herself, there was only more confusion. Thinking back to Lila and the curiosity with which she'd leapt both into her life and into Jakob's lap that same night, Mila wanted to sink her teeth deeper into reality—to be so bold as to claim what she wanted. She felt torn at that moment, for a possibility that was already happening—Jakob, and one that may not be a possibility at all—Baz.

Consumed in thought, Mila heard a knocking on her inner door. It caught a beat in her heart like it was air stuck in her throat—a door was closing shut and she was momentarily stuck feeling the rush of worry making its way into thought-forms. She knew to call upon anything that could help. To turn inward amidst the chaos, to be in liaison with the universe without physical limitations or language. Mila liked thinking of meditation, or similar acts like getting together with friends around tea and tarot, as a way of communing with the divine—something to connect her with the grand beyond. These types of meetings always filled the air with a sense of belonging that were usually unbeknownst to Mila through words. It was a feeling that could not be tapped into unless lived through—to say that one knows of a thing and to be at the centre of its orbit is an entirely different feeling.

A séance was due.

She set up her candles—already melted at the edges—on the living room floor. She put on classical music that altered the fibre of her being when played—it was, of course, playlisted with a title of unrequited love and rain. And, finally, she left out some salt and a blue-eyed pendant to garnish the act of protection against what—who—she was about to summon.

She settled on Lila as the object of her focus, deciding to ask about the Baz in her reality—if there was one at all. She knew that Lila's life would be tainted with desperation—perhaps its truth would not ring the same for Mila, but it was worth a try. With a candle lit to represent Lila, Mila closed her eyes settling into silence, into potentiality. As they blinked open moments later, she saw Lila on the other side of the candle, a mirrored image of herself. She spewed her question without hesitation, not knowing how long she'd be able to maintain the connection since Lila was flickering with the flame.

Lila looked indifferent to the question and spoke of it as casually as possible.

"We used to be a thing. It ended because he could never really make up his mind...and no matter what I tried on him, he was still as wishy-washy as yours probably is."

"What's wrong with him?" Mila asked.

"Maybe, and this is *me* saying it, I am self-aware, you know, and I know you think I am desperate—but just maybe, it's not meant to be. Don't waste your time on him, find something better to do."

Lila's words shocked Mila—and induced guilt. The name-calling was a reflection of herself, and she knew that already, but learning of Lila's self-awareness was a revelatory experience. Lila was going through whatever she was in her own life, similar to Mila or not, but she had decided to take control of the situation. Not letting life happen to her, but for her. And despite some things not working out for her, *she* knew how to "get over it," how to channel her desire to love onto someone else. This was something Mila never considered. She knew she would not be the person to play with free will, but she was not beyond using the energy she so freely spent on Baz elsewhere—she now understood this having seen it play out in Lila's life. Anything that reminded her of him was a gentle, fluttering reminder of the endless possibilities—the pain and the pleasure.

X.

THE STAR(S ALIGN)

Instructed by a merciful teacher, Mila walked into the backroom of a humble studio she had never been to. Buckets of muddy water stood before her—all exuding a sense of tense shoulders and earnest creations. She took to the lone sink witnessing the tiling around the mirror—frayed and chipped on some edges but generally well kept. The sun hit the glazing on the tiles and each shone in their unique way bearing illustrations dissimilar to one another but, somehow, fitting perfectly into a pattern of abstractions. One caught Mila's eye and while lathering her hands with soap, the sound of running water and the chatter from the studio hummed peacefully in her ears. She examined the tile art, the vines that held small, round, red fruit hanging from twirling stems. It was not an image unfamiliar to, say, an Italian restaurant, but it felt foreign amongst the others—it seemed like a real scene. She imagined she could touch it and be transported into a romantic still of chirping birds beyond a darkened room in the early serenity of morning light. Perhaps breakfast would be ready for her downstairs in a garden adjacent to that of Eden with a pool of luscious, almost velvet, water to bathe into, cleanse with, learn the truth from—*would* it all be there?

The running tap water splashed onto her as she instinctively ran one hand atop the other to better wash her hands—the droplets caught her attention and the water drew her back to reality, bringing her out of the physically idling fantasy. She turned it off, tightening it with a firm grip, and dressed herself with a clay-splattered apron.

Taking her seat at a kick-wheel, she tucked her hair behind her ears, wet the plate with a sponge and let the water trickle to the outer edges with a slow spin.

She had not taken the time to go back to a ceramics studio in what felt like the longest Sunday to exist simply because she had been too busy with life. But this itself was life to her—an act of creation beckoning breath. It is a séance of its own, she thought, to materialize an image out of her own mind into a presence—a vessel of energy is a form of alchemy, in the most modern sense of the word—every act of creation objectifies spiritual energy in the thing created[6]. And though a vase was not necessarily Baz-related, she knew she could pour both the stickiness and soreness of knowing him into the art of creating. Getting back to the art would be how she got back to herself, she decided.

*

Mila had come to understand during the week after her séance with Lila that obsession is a fickle love. For she did *love* Baz, but not in the way people typically do—he took her completely out of reality and into grand leaps of potentiality. She had somehow begun to love the distraction of finding reasons to love someone arbitrarily. Her imagination had reigned over their communications, painting them a rosy hue to subdue past hurt. The obsession reeked of desperation—it spilled out onto the streets every time she opened her front door or mouth, not through physical items or words, but rather the constant starvation she had come to live with—the insatiable and vicious creature taking residence within her, call it lust or gluttony. She had mistaken Baz to be the sorcerer, placing her under a spell of sorts, and she was still sure there was something about him that made *him* the object of her desire, but the truth was that he was merely there, and the obsession grew more viscous with each rejection—there is no motivating force stronger than not having what one wants.

Only Alive on Sundays

Monday and Tuesday had passed in a tired episode of autopilot, Wednesday was more hopeful and the air—more crisp. Luna was bustling more than usual. Mila tended to a cast of patrons with a smile on her face and her hands busied with making coffee or taking the contents of left pockets. Thursday, she had seen Jakob and settled into easiness once again. Friday was spent brainstorming how to make the next Sunday her own, how to negotiate the sensitivity and passion treading her livelihood. By Saturday, she had settled on a list of activities—swimming in the stream as the sun rose being one of them—that would rejuvenate her, allow her to be a human of her own accord again. She considered going to the Three Swords Bookshop and getting lost in its aisles, and then consequently getting lost in a book, but she wanted something more physical and less imaginative—she had been inside her mind long enough, she had thought. That evening, she had settled on returning to pottery; its hands-on nature was the exact thing she needed to feel through and release what she had been gripping so intensely.

*

Tracing out the week and landing on the present moment was therapeutic for her—when she did not understand the reason of life, which was often enough, she could at least witness its rhyme. Everything has a pattern and to hear the music in it is enough sometimes, she thought.

During her hour of reflection which was also occupied with chatter amongst new friends, she found a vase half-formed—it was in need of smoothing, shaping, and decorating, but *she* had brought it to life. She knew this vase would hold water in the fridge, and not flowers like she had originally intended. She would drink from it every day and be reminded of the thing she created just to create. Maneuvering a serrated scraper to create ridges resembling waves in water, she pressed into the vase spinning on the wheel. It gave easily, it was just how she imagined it would feel to fall into someone while still maintaining a sense of self—not having to give away all of herself, but finding a cadence that mirrors that of the universe: simple, magical.

Lost in the thought and excitement of having gotten over it, for real this time, she pressed harder into the tool with confidence. Its one edge caught the skin on the outside of her index finger which began to leak small beads of blood. She wiggled her finger, watching the blood move into its crevice.

Mila ran her hand under the tap water examining the wound with her thumb; she grazed the two digits against each other to both soothe and sense the intensity of the incident. The blood was still oozing gently as if breaking into reality for the first time. She considered the sensitivity of human skin—it holds both tension and harmony within it, the constant traffic inside being the most necessary for survival. Order to the chaos.

Her creation was sitting there when she returned from the bathroom once again. It was lonesome without her attention giving it meaning, and though it was finished, it still needed to be removed from the wheel. To preserve the health of her blood, she got it ready for firing with the help of an acquaintance. It was Sunday after all, and Sundays were supposed to be easy. Though a small cut did not take away from the flow, she decided that, for now, the journey could wait[7]. Pauses found her whenever she needed one, and she need not grow mad or angry for the interruption—rather, she was thankful to time itself for showing her where to stop and just witness.

She considered pottery itself to be a masterclass in patience—creations need to go through a process of burning up and surviving before they can be coated with a layer of meaning—colour.

Perhaps they had that in common.

XI.

THE EMPEROR
(HAS NO CLOTHES)[8]

*

Stopping by the market earlier in the morning, Mila had picked up the produce that needed *her* rather than gathering what she had needed. It had been a more intuitive collection of fruits and vegetables—all laid bare amongst one another—calling to the sense of newness within her. She had felt transported back in time, as if gathering berries and nuts amongst other women. There had not been a friend nor foe at the market, but she had still felt she knew everyone there—the routine had finally been set in stone. It had felt like her ancestors were watching her to make sure that she got ingredients for nothing in particular, but rather for colourful cooking. She had not been encumbered with the sight of Baz—or Jakob—and had flowed through the market with an ease only known to women who know not the time of day or year, always lost in the moment of the present.

  A new stand had been there, offering tea blends and spices in overflowing sacs—the stand had changed the entire aroma of the market. The atmosphere was made different by the new possibilities that could come out of the market-goers' creations; perhaps their dishes would now insist on a burning tongue or heightened immunity, perhaps their mornings would now start with a dark cinnamon-y brew. Mila was not about to budge on the coffee that made her days just a bit brighter, but a blend of roses and sugar cubes peppered with yellow and white flowers and short, seemingly stiff, leaves had drawn her in. The label had made Mila chuckle, the words making her think about the different intentions people pour into what they create. *The Love Blend*. It was not so different from Lila's own concoction, she had thought, different ingredients were present, sure, but the idea was the same—to curate an energy that disrupts the rules of reality. Mila had decided tea in the afternoon would not be so bad and bought some, assuming that she could perhaps offer it to the non-coffee drinkers that stop by Luna Monday through Saturday.

*

Mila insisted to the voice inside her head that she would paint the vase from last week blue, tiled with darker blue and some sort of flowering design. The voice insisted back that it must be pink, clouded with paler pink and little yellow suns. She had made herself an iced version of *The Love Blend* for her walk over to the studio since the heat of the season was still presenting itself as sweat beads on her skin. It still felt like summer and although it was not officially fall, September had arrived and the leaves had changed colour—September was a melancholy that the heat had not yet been familiarized with.

Greeting the instructor and other pottery-on-a-Sunday enthusiasts with a gentle smile, Mila threw her apron on quickly while darting toward the fired ceramics, ready to add a touch of colour that would bring life to their hardened, pale shells. She found her vase, but it was not as she would wish it to be. It was broken at the hip in three different pieces—she smoothed over the sharp edges that could not withstand the heat of the kiln and felt a similar fire beginning in the pit of her stomach.

She was angry at the outcome of something she had poured herself into a week prior—for it to only end up as mere pieces of a vase that could not be used felt spiteful to her. She considered that the piece may have already been cracked in some way prior to the kiln; the fire had perhaps just made it more pronounced, eventually ripping it apart with an invisible force. But it felt more personal than that.

Only Alive on Sundays

Since the creation was the pinnacle of her getting "over" Baz, Mila thought him to be the culprit. He always showed up unannounced and it was not beyond him to think of her in the small of night—perhaps it was his grip on her that had destroyed her creation as it held energetic ties to both him and her. Mila's madness violently grew stronger as if it was a flower blooming faster than it ought to—to her, it felt like she wasn't supposed to get over him at all since each opportunity to do so was followed by an event or encounter tinged with abnormality.

She sat on a stool, holding the pieces in her hand, staring in disbelief at Baz's capabilities. She was sure he had colluded with the universe in some way to keep her stuck. The instructor passed by and, sensing the grief Mila was enduring, she kindly noted that there's always more clay to go around. Mila feigned a smile and was about to thank her for the sentiment when her phone started vibrating in her pocket. *Basil.*

She had never before gotten a phone call from Baz. Reckoning it either serious or out of some pure omniscient knowledge he possessed, she answered.

"Hi."

"Hey, Mila, listen I really need something from you—Luna—today."

She wanted to tell him it was closed but her curiosity was more piqued than her desire to mourn what never was.

"What is it?"

"I don't actually know, but I kind of just need something."

"Like a sign?" she asked

"Something like that."

Mila felt a certain wrath at his thoughtlessness. She knew that he knew nothing about her vase or the fact that she was actively trying to get over him—over nothing—but it was easier to make him a demon and herself a victim. To be mad at him was a reason to be okay with herself, okay with the patterns she constantly found herself weaving into. She did wonder what sort of sign Baz could possibly need, but she knew that she herself needed a sign more desperately.

"It's Sunday. I can help you tomorrow, but it's Sunday and Luna is closed on Sundays."

"Oh," he said, "okay. That's alright, maybe tomorrow, then," he said.

She thanked him for understanding, and they parted ways—in the most distant sense of the phrase.

Her phone was now lying beside the broken pieces of the vase, and she felt proud of herself—she was allowing her heart to mend by denying him access to her whenever he wanted it. The curiosity about what he needed was going to kill her, it could have been an opportunity for her to *see* him, *know* him, finally, but the restraint she took to not give in was applaudable—she sat up more poised after taking such pride in herself. The instructor walked over offering a warm smile—she had perhaps sensed the urgency that the vase offered Mila—and, winking, placed a kit in front of her: *Kintsugi*.

Mila was familiar with the Japanese art of mending what is broken with gold-dusted lacquer. She remembered her mom's plate at Luna. It was broken at the chest, but the delicate lines of gold gave it more meaning than it would have held had it been presented whole—it was an optimistic placeholder for a beating life, full of flaws and all.

The technique, and the art itself being revamped, is an appreciation for the way that, sometimes, things do not go to plan. Being ready for life to fall apart, not wishing for it to, but knowing that eventually some things do, Mila thought, is the meaning of strength, in the truest sense of the word. And mending what falls victim to life's push and pull is an act of giving—finding—deeper meaning *in* the thing, in what it implies about humanity itself.

Only Alive on Sundays

While glazing two ridges and pressing the shoulder of the vase to the lip, Mila considered that cracks can also hold things together—they can create a composite of meanings. What was once broken has the ability to pull experience and memory into the same plane of existence. Mila would now have a vase adorned with gold all throughout, but it would also remind her of the universe's push for more discipline, of how she denied Baz one day over her own needs, of how the very thing made to channel her love for Baz was now a signifier of her self-love. It took great strength to be able to say no to him—this, the vase would not let her forget.

The mending of things is what makes them potent, she thought.

She thought back to how Jakob had quickly mended their relationship post name-slip. And she knew he was only able to do so because of his lack of knowledge regarding the situation. She felt like an outsider in their connection, like she had pushed herself away by remaining ambiguous. It was her turn to mend what was seemingly good but had a suffocating hold on just one of them. She needed to be able to fully breathe again.

Mila left the mended vase in the studio to be glazed with shine once more, forgoing any pattern as to make the gold the only thing of importance. She showed up at Jakob's front door just as the sky was mocking itself with colours unbeknownst to it during the day. He rattled the door open, looking dishevelled, but a grin appeared on his face with the realization of Mila's presence gracing him. Her arms were spotted with gold specks, and a little stain adorned her cheek, too. He smiled, bringing her in for a kiss on the forehead—his height made the interaction the only one possible in their natural postures.

"Let's get a drink," she told him.

"Sure, I'm supposed to go down to Inferno's later," he smiled, "why not make it sooner?"

She was pleased he was able to be spontaneous—that being the least of any Tweed's capabilities.

They walked down to a bar called Inferno's and sat down on a velvet loveseat coloured a hue adjacent to that of the tiles in Jakob's bathroom. The wall behind them was painted dark red, frames of gold paintings illustrated a contrast between what simply is and what is simply on display. They ordered their drinks—he, a house beer named Limbo, and she, something to tame, perhaps mediate, the anger of the day and the flow she desired to be in: Greed.

Mila excused herself to the bathroom to practice in the mirror what she was about to tell Jakob. She peered past the doors and noticed the mending theme of the day was still on track. The tiles had been torn out and, although some of the wine-red ones were still intact, the rest were bare—not necessarily exposing an empty wall, but instead, black cement. It seemed as though the wall would make space for her if she plunged her fingers into the membrane of its darkness, embracing her whole. Temptation brought her fingers to the wall. There was no indication of the place being under construction, but this was definitely new. She considered how unfinished the quiet bathroom looked, and perhaps that was the point—this place was always a work in progress—to expect anything else would be a sin on one's own part. Mila retracted her fingers, and her sense of exploration, she had purpose waiting for her just beyond the door. She practiced her lines, mouthing Baz's name slowly so as to not get distracted by its feel in her mouth when she utters it to Jakob once again. She smoothed down her skirt, washed her hands, and made her way back to Jakob. She knew admitting what she was about to would be the final step in getting over it.

She gutted herself in the name of truth.

She let him in—the naming of lust in the moment had not been a mere accident, but an intrusion, too. She let

Only Alive on Sundays

him in on how Baz had come to see her after the market two weeks ago, how she had *had* feelings for him for years, never acting upon them, or telling him via anything but jokes and letters never sent to him but kept for her or the ether's personal gain. She revealed how she was always laying out a web—until she started having feelings for Jakob, the web became unintentional at that point.

"I wanted to tell you because it's important to me that you know. So that anything between us doesn't become tainted by this, by him."

He stiffened, sitting taller in the seat shared by the two of them.

"I kind of knew," Jakob replied, "But I get it. We don't choose who we love, or lust, I guess."

"What makes you think it's lust?" she asked him.

"How could it be love?"

"I guess it can't be, not in the typical sense of the word," she said.

They sat side by side, silence taking a seat between them. She asked him how he knew.

"He noted that he had harboured certain feelings for you in the past. But he ultimately gave me his blessing. I'm uncertain what that's good for now, though."

She felt an uneasiness start at the bottom of her spine that shudderingly made its way up to her crown. The sensation turned into a thought—such a conversation happening between the two men seemed disgusting, derogatory in a way. It made her almost instantaneously "get over it," knowing that Baz had felt that he had the right to bless Jakob with her. After a quiet moment, she realized she would do the same if the roles were reversed: when someone senses the person they care about falling for someone else, doing what's best for them is getting out of the way.

"How do you feel, knowing my side?" she asked him.

"Honestly, really good. I had an inkling there was something going on ever since my party. But neither of you said anything until today. I think it took a lot of courage on your part especially."

She thanked him with a smile.

"Now that you've told me, it feels like you're ready to start," he said, looking like he was pondering if she knew what he meant, "With me."

"I am," she said.

Deciding to continue the honesty streak, Mila took a sip of her drink and looked Jakob in the eyes for a few seconds longer than she ever had.

"Your grandfather's painting. Why did you throw it away in the Luna trash?"

"Okay, so, to—um, understand that," he also took a sip which made his lips shiny, Mila noticed, "he painted it for me. But I was really young and it was daunting. It kind of represented me, but it was suffocating. Like I had to constantly be the light at the end of the tunnel. It was strict."

Mila felt that knowing him before was a preface to knowing him now. Jakob had to be the one to hold everything together and maybe that was why he was a Tweed. Perhaps he was born into it, perhaps he took it on. It might have been his destiny.

"Then, he died," he continued, "and I felt like I needed it back, which is when I walked into Luna five weeks ago."

"We yearn for what we fear for[9]," Mila said.

He nodded, knowingly.

"I had it for a few days and," he said, then paused to think.

Short love, Mila thought.

"Every time I tried to get rid of it, it ended up in some cupboard or on a wall in my house," he continued, now more excitedly, "But! but, but but! I thought to throw it away at Luna, and it worked!"

"Genius," she replied, knowing that the trash at Luna was a black hole for all the impurities of life, love, and life again—the things not meant for mending. She should have put her letters for Baz there, she realized, though retrospection was in her favour at this particular hour.

Mila considered that her summoning skills were up to par with the painting since Baz waltzed in just as she and Jakob had bookended the serious nature of their conversation with a cheers. Baz looked caught-off-guard seeing Mila there, he seemed unprepared as if he was walking into a shift he had forgotten he signed up for.

"That's why I was going to come here later," Jakob said, standing to greet Baz.

"Hey, guys," Baz said, sitting down in the single arm chair at their table. He ordered the Gluttony on tap, and it made Mila smile inwardly—reality always reflected her inner world.

She told them about the vase fiasco. Jakob told them he had been lesson-planning for the wrong grade level all day. It seemed that Baz was about to admit to his crisis as he likely noticed the softness growing between the three of them, but Jakob interrupted by saying that he still had a lot of work to do before tomorrow.

"I'll come help you maybe?" she asked him.

"Stay," he whispered, "be friends."

She stood up and gave him a kiss—Baz watched, not looking entirely pleased or displeased with the situation.

Watching Jakob leave, she sat back down and turned to Baz. There was not a twinge of pain in her heart. Rather, the easiness of friendship settled in between them like the first gentle snowfall of a long winter season that was not yet there.

XII.

(POETIC) JUSTICE

The next day was, of course, Monday.
Mila rolled out of bed with her brain not feeling completely secure in her skull. There was a pin-balling within her that one would typically associate with the excessive consumption of drinks flowing in between friends in celebration of something grand. Though she and Baz likely toasted to different occasions the night prior, it was official. They were officially nothing but friends. On her part, at least.
Mila gulped down a tall glass of water at room temperature while standing barefoot in her kitchen. She wiggled her toes on the cold ground, each embracing the earth beneath them as to prolong the initial greeting between morning and a human body. It was early, and Mila would have to go open Luna in two or three hours, so she took advantage of the early rise with a shower that paid respect to the gods—if there were any—of steam and heat.
The tiles in Mila's bathroom were sweating, perhaps crying. They seemed to mirror the weather outside—the rain came down violently, daring everyone to stay home with an excuse found folded in the crevices of their mind. The blue inside, Mila noticed, was glazed with condensation, resembling the sky or the sea—its indistinguishable depth was a distorted reality. Mila's ability to breathe was unstifled by the warm air filling the room. The ache in her head had not ceased, but felt more manageable. It was Monday and Luna would be open for business. Right after some coffee.

Only Alive on Sundays

Mila changed out of her rain boots once inside the shop. She began organizing the odd pieces of antiques found in places they should not be. She thought to put on music while clearing away the past week's energy, but the rain made for an enchanting score, and so she stayed humming the rhythm of nature synchronizing with humanity. Mila considered it an all-encompassing void that so many of the waking hours pour into mundanities that sustain the unawake hours. The void is full of distractions and obsessions that give it meaning. The void itself gets mistaken for life, for days of the week that pass by nonchalantly singing tunes and slogans to chase what feels *right*.

Mila had her gaze fixed on an amulet that belonged to the shop at this point—no one had bought it since she'd started working there, but she never thought to get rid of it. It fit the shop, perhaps it contained the energy of Luna itself and no one bat an eye at its curves because they somehow knew it was not for sale. She was about to give it meaning to appease her sense of dread, but was distracted by the chime of entrance, the whoosh of the portal sinking into reality, and the crisp sound of rain seeping into the shop while the door was momentarily open as to welcome an old lady.

"Good morning, dear," the old lady said in greeting.

"Hi there!"

"Mind if I just have a look around?"

"Sure thing, we have a sale on the section in the back corner, if anything there piques your interest," Mila told her.

Setting the groundwork for the lady to find what she was likely looking for, Mila turned on the kettle to make a cup of *The Love Blend* for Luna's current target.

Mila set the aromatic mug down in front of the woman who was now knitting with silver needles and a ball of purple yarn. Her tools had a pattern carved into them that Mila could not identify. The old lady made no gesture as to thank Mila, so she backed away leaving the lady to it. It seemed hypnotic, meditative for the old lady to be weaving a pattern into reality with her own hands. Mila considered how love is the same—she always went back to love—it is a pattern brought out between people with their very own hands or words or acts. The pattern could reign toxic, a murkier green, or sentimental, a sweeter green found in serene lowlands. Obsession and love have too many similarities, Mila thought. Perhaps the old lady loved her hobby, perhaps she was obsessed with the escape it offered. She was too deep in the movements to notice anything else, and Mila could not tell which shade of green the old lady was overtaken by. Her fervent dedication to the item she was knitting was a prayer to the holiest act there is—time spent in communion with a story being weaved. Love is a story, Mila thought.

    The entirety of the workday marking the beginning of the week was spent in service. Mila helped a record number of patrons find the thing their hearts desired—her own mind dared not drift toward desire as she was too busy gratifying the needs of others. For once, she had not been distracted. This was a state of being she was coming to know as if starting life on the right foot—and this, she could not confuse with a void. She was not sucked into her work, rather, she was learning the dance of give and take—it was not the solo performance she had grown used to.

    She was beginning to close up the shop, tidying the wayward items people had left behind, when she noticed the old lady was still knitting in the corner. Mila let her know that she would be closing the shop soon, but the lady made no indication to acknowledge her. Mila gently approached her, laying a hand on her shoulder to grab her attention, but no such attention transpired. It seemed the old lady could spend eternity knitting her increasingly long scarf. Mila placed her hand over the lady's, slowing the speed with which she was knitting and the lady finally looked up at Mila's face.

"Sorry, dear, have I been here all day?" she asked.

"Most of it. What are you making anyway?" Mila responded.

"Heavens, I have no clue," she said, "I must have been deep in thought thinking of days gone by."

"How poetic," Mila confirmed, "Were the memories what you needed?"

"I," she paused, "have no clue. I was lost in it, dear."

"Would you like to buy those knitting needles?" Mila offered, hoping the old lady would at least walk out of Luna with something other than a wasted day.

"No, I have no need for them," the old lady answered.

Mila's stomach swirled with an unfamiliar sense of knowing that she could not make sense of logically. Despite the discomfort, she helped the old lady outside. See you never, she thought—getting rid of the old lady would surely take away the feeling of her gut being wrung out. This viscerally intimidating instance is a symptom of being afraid of the future—it is always a sense of missing out on the world, on something necessary for survival, that trickles in when the fear of not knowing settles in, Mila thought. It is also the mind deciding that there is something out there that *should* be known with words and thoughts. That is, of course, despite the body already knowing in a language similar to that of fruits ripening, of learning through trial and mostly error, of the bitterness of a lesson learned.

Mila stepped outside breathing in the now slow rain that landed softly on the ground like gentle dew on flower petals. The tension within her also slowed, her gut no longer felt like it was being drained of its blood. She locked the door to the shop to get back home to her own door—and her loveseat, her bathroom tiles, her bed, her nightstand, her journal, her glass of water, her self.

The old lady's summoning of her personal void penetrated Mila's thoughts on the walk home. The lady had gone somewhere not quite here nor there, maybe she had slipped into the universe. But she had been stuck—immobile, seemingly uninspired. Had it not been for Mila's prompting—would she have ever snapped out of it? She could have spent an entire week there, Mila thought. Monday through to the next, in search of what the end of knitting would bring her, if anything at all. Perhaps the knitting made her come to terms with memories of the past physically rather than mentally. Whatever her past was, it was not worthy of buying the needles, of holding onto them to savour what they could offer to the present—that, for Mila, was new.

The old lady had gotten "over it" much faster than Mila was able to.

XIII.

THE HERMIT

An exhausting week of work had passed. It seemed that the whole world had appeared in front of Luna's steps, each person begging to get over something from their own lives in little whispers made to antiques and grazes on dusty shelves. The amulet however, remained unperturbed. No one showed interest in it despite its obvious allure—it was a life source of its own, Mila was sure. The shop was not a lucrative business, but it did not matter, for Mila was busy and people were becoming who they were meant to be— bloodlines were healed, and stories of shame and love unraveled. Luna always took care of itself.

On this beloved Sunday, Mila slept in like she was re-discovering the concept. Dreams came to her as if they were the revelations offered to people who occupy the liminal space between humanity and godhood. Her mind-TV was turned off in sleep, but it took on another role offering secrets only known to her psyche, however cryptic they may be. She was gloriously comfortable in her bed— the duvet softening the air, the mattress beneath her sinking her deeper into another reality. Her senses were muffled and so her mind had the opportunity to rest, to unravel, to take care.

In her dream, or perhaps vision, Lila sat at the chair the old lady had been in nearly a week ago. She knit, while in reverie herself, but her hands dripped of blood and the creation, a scarf, was seemingly alive—a pulsing body of tragedy. Lila's yarn was not the typical type, it was thick, and real. Mila looked down to the source—the bodies of

Jakob and Baz gutted, but the two were very much alive. They spoke and joked amongst themselves while Lila took more and more slack from their intestines. They seemed undisturbed by the event, but Lila mindlessly wove from the two of them a neat scarf, joining their flesh into one new, whole, being. Mila was merely observing the scene in the dream. For the men, the situation was normal, for Lila, she seemed unaware of it entirely; until she reached her hand out to Mila. Mila took it, blood now staining her own hands. She led Mila through the portal section, both of them squeezing through the letter slot seemingly atom by atom.

    On the other side, Mila's apartment took shape, her furnishings slowly coming to their natural resting places. *You're home now,* Lila notified her. Except she was not. The floor was soft on impact and the bathroom tiles—they were not tiles at all, they were a slab of flesh moving like a beating heart, though notably in their normal pale blue colour as if to disguise who they really were. In a sudden panic, Mila realized there was no door for entry or exit into the apartment. This could not be home, Mila thought—for some place to be the sanctity of home, there must be an outside to seek shelter from. If there is no escape, it is not a home—it is a prison. Mila's heart thumped to the rhythm of the "tiles" in the bathroom as Lila stood in her apartment with an eerie smile. She looked as if she was a real estate agent showing her around the place, waiting for a confirmation of if Mila loved it and if she would sign the lease. Sweat beads started to form on Mila's forehead, and in a delirious tossing and turning, she awoke from the nightmare and entered back into the realm of wakefulness.

    She sat up in bed—her back was dripping dampness and her sleep-clothes clung to her body—she looked around to confirm she was in her own, actual, apartment. Her breaths slowed with confirmation, and though she knew her mind was processing what her body

Only Alive on Sundays

had sensed, she was grateful that she could escape the world building itself inside her head.

With an ache in her chest, disturbed by Lila once again, she wondered why she couldn't have a normal life—why both her waking hours and sleeping ones revolved around men. She knew Lila was obsessed, and that she herself could be obsessed, but her whole life was being dictated by the desire to be desired, it seemed. Mila took the compliance of both Baz and Jakob in the dream to be a self-fulfilling oracle of sorts. They were being consumed at their own detriment, their sense of self and autonomy diminishing with each turn of Lila's wrist. Perhaps it was the men's desire to be desired, too, reflected in the dream. Desire was at the root of everything, and no man, woman, person, can ever escape—we want the wanting, Mila thought.

Mila went to her bathroom and placed her palms on the tiles—the dream had made them out to be a character, alive in their simple act of existence. She ran her thumb in between the tiles, down the caulk. She stood there for a moment longer than a moment—she let the tiles sink into her skin, become one with the pads of her fingers and rearrange the swirls of identity embedded into her. They did not pulse or move in any fashion, but Mila sensed a pain held within them, or herself. Their purpose was to decorate a seemingly plain wall, give it personality, act as protection, breathe life into the room. Mila knew the tiles did not *feel* a certain way, but they had communicated to her what she already knew. That she was alive and going through the motions without giving much thought to what was beneath the surface. Suddenly, she wanted to check her front door, to see if it was there or not, if it would allow her to leave or not. She nearly ran across her apartment in her determination to swing it open. It did not give, and she sensed her heart drop into her stomach for a split second, but all she could manage was a laugh—the door was simply

87

locked. She unlocked it, pulling at the knob a second time, and it revealed to her the reality of the hallway just beyond.

She was standing at the threshold and knew not what to do with her day at this point. She could go back to sleep, but the sheets needed to be washed before any comfort could be felt in between them now. She thought could go to the market, but she felt she needed more time alone before she ran into another person she knew. She settled on her vase—she could go pick it up, the present moment likely being the perfect time.

She threw on a coat and walked to the studio while considering why the ether beyond the letter slot at Luna would lead her to an un-homely home—perhaps it was to say that it all comes from within, perhaps it was to make no sense at all. Maybe it was to act as another pause in her life.

She arrived at the studio unintentionally disheveled and picked up her vase. It was organically simple with its golden ridges winking at her when the sun caught it just right, and she thought it to be the most eloquent statement of all. She walked home with it pressed to her chest admiring its imperfections. Turning the corner to her street, she noticed Baz leaning on her door—he mirrored the pose of the vase with its handle perched on its hip.

"Hi," she said.

"Hey," he replied, "I'm on my way to Jakob's. Let's go surprise him, I know he had a rough week at work."

Mila was dumbfounded—she had not seen much of Jakob the past week, he being busy at work, too. She had no idea it had been a rough week for him. She did not want to physically go check on him despite wanting to be there for him—she felt as though she needed to find her footing.

"You go, I have to sort some things out. Maybe I'll see you guys later tonight?"

"Sure, see you," he said, walking away.

XIV.

THE HIEROPHANT

Mila found herself at Jakob's door nearing the end of her Sunday of solitude. She had insisted on getting out of the house after spending her entire day there alone and maybe in love. The air was flowing throughout her apartment, the windows were spread open as if they were a tasting board for the sweet air, and the universe danced with her through wind and light. The spectacle had lasted several hours, leaving Mila exhausted by the end of the day. She wanted to relax, to let go and let live, and she knew the way to do that now was to be with friends, in silence or laughter. Mila now wanted to check up on Jakob. It seemed odd to her that he would not communicate the troubles he was having to her but, rather, to Baz. Perhaps they had spoken and it was mentioned in passing. Although, Mila was surpassingly harder to reach these days—her nose was down her soul on Sundays and down Luna every other day.

She knocked on Jakob's door, thinking it better to not call ahead, to regress to pre-phonelines, to skip the mediation of asking if she could see him and to just announce herself with her presence. The door crept open seeming distracted by the energy inside as if it was harder to push open because people had been getting along just beyond it. Baz surfaced when the door fully opened; he seemed more surprised to see Mila there than she was to see him still at Jakob's house, hours and hours after he'd said he was meeting him. Mila realized they had spent the whole day together and felt a tiny sword pierce her heart—in a seaweed green hue—when Jakob interrupted the silence from the same couch Mila had melted into a month ago.

"Mila?" he said with surety but also in a way to ask for confirmation.

She looked at Baz.

"He said he just knew you were going to show up any moment now," Baz explained.

She shook off the green feeling renewed with purpose and entered through the threshold, once again sensing that she was being initiated into whatever space was left inside of *their* romance.

Mila gave Jakob a kiss and sat beside him. Baz picked up whatever conversation they were likely having before she arrived, and Mila tuned it out. She was instead tuning into the heaviness of Jakob's arm around her and its delicate balance of gentle and territorial. Mila was lost on the conversation, and though they accepted her presence, they did not seem too keen on explaining the context, and so Mila pulled out a joint and a towel from her tote bag. She held up the joint to lure the men—their noses followed the scent as if they were dogs in a cartoon, each giving her puppy eyes, asking for permission to devour it whole, salivating at the mouth just at the thought of getting high.

This time it was Mila who announced the game, "Race you guys there."

They all took a pause, each looking at one another to evaluate the situation, and with a break in laughter, they all got up to run to the backdoor. The game had gotten more competitive now—each opponent obstructed another as to get there first. There would be no prize or a punishment of any sort, had anyone been last or first, but it was fun to act like children momentarily, before the adult of the week, Monday, came home again. Mila threw her sweater over Baz's head, Jakob yanked on her arm, Baz held onto Jakob's leg while on the ground. This was the foreplay to their playscape: the hot tub that held so much history between all of them in such a short amount of time.

The jets whirred in effervescent circles—the light from the floor of the hot tub approached the surface as if it wanted to break open into the air and reveal something previously unknown. Mila took its lead and broached the little bit of information she had been given.

"How was work this week?"

Neither answered at first as it was not obvious who Mila was addressing. But Baz decided he would take the lead.

"Mine was alright, had to deal with a few annoying agents. That's what we were talking about before you came. I think I want to start working with some athletes, some of the sports agents we work with don't have a clue what they're doing."

Mila was excited to see Baz's interest in this new possibility. He rarely spoke of his job, and she always thought of him as someone who does the mundane just to coast by in life, but she was proud of him for wanting to do something he seemed to like.

"That's awesome news," she said, passing him the joint, "Congrats on your new-found love!"

Baz rolled his eyes and gladly took the joint to his lips. Mila's eyes lingered on his inhale—when she turned to Jakob to hear about his week, she found him already looking at her, perhaps noticing how her eyes were batting low and staying on lips they had no place in doing so.

He began to answer, taking the joint from Baz.

"My students are... completely disengaged," he said, taking a big inhale himself.

"They don't care about the books I want to teach them, and that's to be expected, they're only in high school, but they're so different from the kids I had last year. It makes it harder for me to want to teach them," he said with a full stop, as if contemplating how to get his pupils interested again.

He took another long inhale and passed the joint back to Mila. She took it, considering an answer.

"Did you ask them what they want to read?" Baz asked.

"Sure, but they don't know what they don't know, you know?" Jakob said, already sounding high.

Mila chuckled, choking on the last bit of smoke in her lungs, "Make them read something gruesome, keep them on their toes," she said, after clearing her throat.

"Not a bad idea, actually," Jakob replied, bringing her head in closer to himself to plant a kiss on her forehead.

"How was your week, Mila?" Baz asked.

"Busy. So insanely busy at Luna. I think I saw everyone who lives in this town and their parents, and their dead relatives, too."

"Maybe someone wrote about the portal somewhere online?" Jakob asked.

"Probably," Baz added.

They continued their chatter, each speaking of whatever concerned them—offering advice the best they could—until silence was due. Each of the trio took up space on the walls of the hot tub, closing their eyes in relaxation, enjoying the company of quiet friendship. The water felt easy against Mila's skin, she knew the sensation to be that of surrender. She let the water envelop her with its holiness, and she did the same unto the water. It was an act of surrender to be here with Baz and Jakob—and she liked it all too well.

Distracted by a train of thought calling her back to her dream, which she was about to announce to the men, Baz interrupted the silence with a giggling never heard by the other two in his company. Mila peered her eyes open, as did they, to find Jakob grazing Baz's feet with his toes. They all burst out into laughter—Mila especially could not speak straight through the guffaws spilling out of her mouth.

"I thought they were your feet!" Jakob claimed with a hint of exaggerated passion which he was just starting to express himself with.

They finally slowed on the laughter, "I liked it," Baz said.

"I did, too," Mila added, winking.

Mila sunk back into her moment of meditation while the men continued to speak. She heard words and knew what they meant, but they were strung in such foreign ways that meaning could not be construed. Perhaps she didn't care to understand, for she knew them and they knew her, and that was enough. But she wondered suddenly, did they *really* know her? She wanted to tell them about the dream, and so she opened her eyes and put their conversation on hold to spill her own guts about the joining of theirs in a scarf knit by an alternate-reality version of herself—to initiate *them* into her psyche.

They were on the edge of their seats listening to the bloody details.

"And we were willing participants?" Baz asked, intrigued, maybe teasing.

She nodded.

The two men looked at each other and laughed, seeming pleased at the dream, or her re-telling of it.

"Sounds like you think we're made of the same cloth, Mila," Jakob said seriously like an accusation, but his tilted smile gave him away.

She enjoyed watching them be amused by what she had to say. They were closer together now, acting as an audience, and she—a one-woman-show.

"You both know you're very similar," she responded.

They nodded in agreement, their heads even moved in unison. Perhaps it was her high wearing off, but time seemed to slow and the water being pushed back and forth was taking its own time making it to the walls of the hot tub, splashing on the men's bare chests and then circling back around Mila's body. She knew the night would end soon, but she didn't want it to. She wanted this to go on forever, for every day to be Sunday. She wanted the rest of the days of the week to mean something else. And she felt a sense of hesitation, for she wanted all that and did not at the same time. She knew tomorrow had to be Monday, and yet, she still dreaded it. For Sunday to offer this *short love*, there needs to be something outside of it as contrast, she thought.

[Handwritten annotation: Sorta binary opposition. Can one opposite exist without its opposite?]

XV.

THE (STAR-CROSSED) LOVERS

"What if I don't get the job?" Baz asked while he and Mila were waiting for their drinks at Inferno's. Jakob had excused himself to the bathroom.
"Okay, but what if you do?" Mila answered.
"I'll have to start over."
"Then you'll start over, it'll be okay," she reassured him.
"Honestly don't know if I have that in me."
"You're never going to get anything you want if you're scared of having it."
"He's scared of having what?" Jakob asked, passing between the two to get to his seat.
"Literally everything. He's Mr. Self-saBAZtage," Mila said.
Baz laughed, though it seemed that the joke did not land with Jakob. His face was more stern than when Mila had first entered the bar—she had walked into quite a beautiful scene, the men sitting on the love-seat, seemingly discussing nothing of significance yet appearing to be swept up in the casualness of conversation afforded only to a first date.
It was early in the evening, and although a regular Sunday, Baz seemingly thought it the most opportune of times for a double date.

*

Jakob had proposed the idea to Mila on Thursday, noting that it would help ease the tension for Baz, and she had agreed. That was what friends were for, anyway, she had thought. She had pushed aside the weight of the letter arriving the day after, on Friday—blank as was typical these past weeks.

*

And so, they were waiting at Inferno's for a girl named Donya to show up.

Baz was out of touch with his surroundings picking at the label on his beer. Mila assumed he was consumed by the rockiness of his work situation and, perhaps, having an existential moment due to the conversation they were just having.

"Nervous, are we?" Jakob joked.

"Only when—" the rest of what Mila assumed was a joke in blossom was cut short by Donya's entrance.

Donya was beautiful, in the most human sense of the word. She was not dissimilar to Mila in composition and hair, but she seemed earthier—as if she were the dirt and trees herself. Baz stood up to greet her, they all exchanged casual hellos. The quad rearranged themselves for sake of better communication: Baz across Mila, she beside Jakob, and Donya diagonal Mila.

The night went on tenderly—Jakob and Mila broached subjects they never had before like love and god, macaroni and which type of cheese it best suited, Baz and Donya. Her and Jakob's coupling was easy, for maybe it did not make sense, but sense was not a prerequisite to coming together. She was deep in this thought, the most innately human of them all—the preoccupation with love, falling in and out of it—when she noticed everyone else at the table laughing. She had lost herself to the moment, and not in it, and now felt like an outsider watching a cozy home beyond glass windows during winter. The smiles on their faces made heat rise between them—the square of humans formed an aura not to be perturbed. Mila gathered herself by listening with more intention now as to join in.

"So I told my students that we'd read the book *because* it sucked, and it worked!" Jakob was explaining, his typically more composed tone completely out of sight.

"Next time, try assigning something scandalous," Donya told him, "that'll do the trick!"

"Are you a teacher, too?" Mila jumped in.

"Ninth grade," Baz filled her in.

Donya shot Baz a look as to notify him that she did not enjoy being spoken for.

The Tweeds began discussing their strategies, and Mila looked to Baz for an explanation since she had just disappeared into her own world momentarily. Baz shrugged and offered to go get everyone the next round of drinks.

"I'll come with you," Mila answered.

At the bar, Baz ordered two Limbos, and two Heresys. Mila had her back to the bar and was looking at their table.

"Those two are sure hitting it off, hmm?" Mila teased.

She locked eyes with Jakob and he delivered her the kindest smile she had seen from him thus far—her heart sank, she felt bad having expressed aloud what was simply a thought running through her mind.

"I'm sure they just don't get to geek out about their jobs with friends at the bar normally."

"So, what do you think of her?"

"I like her," Baz said, "But I don't think we're such a good match."

"Okay, Mr. Self-saBAZtage" she teased him.

Baz laughed at her reference and shook his head in mock disappointment.

"Alright, alright," he said while making a hand gesture as if to say let's stop this joke here.

He grabbed all the drinks from the bar in both his hands before Mila had an opportunity to offer help. She eyed how his fingers spread to make room for the necks of the bottles between his digits as they walked back to their table. She was transported to a parallel moment that carried the same weight—when she was waiting for Jakob to open the door to his place after the situation with the masks. His hands had contrasted the solidity of the front door, and then he had later placed them on her wet back, using them to bring her in closer. She felt a butterfly form in her throat, and like before, she was sucked out of the moment into a void she could only categorize as the nesting doll of desire.

Baz perhaps entered his own, though different, void as Jakob and Donya *did* now seem like they were hitting it off.

Another round was proposed after the previous was quickly consumed, but Mila wanted to escape the tension in the room.

"I think I'll head home," she announced, grabbing her sweater.

"I'll walk you home," Jakob told her.

They all found themselves outside the bar expressing their goodbyes. A lull filled in the space between conversation as the wind howled around them. It seemed nobody wanted to part ways, despite members of the group actually wanting to. There was an energy pulling them into one another, forming a web of confusing connections.

"Well," Donya finally said, "I'm this way."

"Bye," Mila said again.

"I'll walk you home?" Baz offered her.

"Sure," she said.

They trekked off and Mila and Jakob still remained at the door staring at each other.

"Let's go?" Jakob asked.

"Yours," she replied.

"Alright," he said, "mine."

Only Alive on Sundays

Jakob proposed they pass by the Three Swords Bookshop—he told Mila that he wanted to show her something in the shop window. So, they took the long way home—despite being tired and needing to wake early on the Monday fast approaching them. They peered in through the window with cupped hands and their faces glued to the glass as to block out light from the street. Inside, the books were organized by gruesome themes like "death by love" or "melodrama" or "painful, but in a good way." Mila noticed their tagline under the shop's sign: "The most heart-wrenching bookstore!"

"Why would someone go into a bookstore intended to make them feel bad?" she posed to Jakob with slight judgement in her voice.

"I assume it's not to feel bad—more so to feel alive," he said.

She pondered that for a moment and saw a truth in it—to feel through the spectrum of emotions is to be alive, to become frantic about decisions and indecisions—visions and revisions that spread across the evening sky[10]—is to experience a wound in the heart and to become even more alive.

"Let's come back later," Mila said now with a desire to truly get lost in between those shelves and find something that would reflect back to her the same ideas.

She wondered why, or what exactly, he'd wanted to show her, but made no question of it.

"Don't drink the coffee though, it's really bad," Jakob said, wrapping his arm around her as they turned to walk away.

They entered his home, chatter filling the space between them and the idle air in his house. Once inside, Mila noticed a blank piece of paper in his foyer. She recognized it to be one of the ones she receives straight from the ether. She wondered if it was because she was thinking of him, or Donya was.

"What's this?" she asked.

"No idea, second one I've gotten this week."

So it was on her behalf or maybe Baz's, she joked to herself.

"Hot tub?" Jakob proposed.

"I'm really tired," Mila answered.

"Not very like you," he said.

Mila was about to take that as an insult, somehow, but was honestly very tired.

"I know," she said, "Can I just have some tea?"

"Why don't you go get ready for bed and I'll bring some up."

She was nestled in his sheets—looking as if she had just been born, as if discovering life for the first time—taking a position intended for babies.

"Hey, let's have the tea in the living room," Jakob said, noticing she was still awake and holding eye contact with him when he came into his bedroom.

And Mila was, again, honestly very tired, and perhaps that is why she took Jakob's proposition to be inconsiderate.

"I'm trying to sleep," she told him bluntly.

"And I am trying to do something nice. Can you also try?" he replied.

"Try?" she questioned.

"I know you care about me, I do. I also see how you look at Baz, but can you just try a little harder with me?"

She felt guilty—she knew exactly what he meant, but her tiredness was making her stubborn.

"I," she paused, "I don't look at Baz like anything."

"Come to the living room for tea," he asserted.

She got up reluctantly.

Only Alive on Sundays

In the living room, he had prepared a fort for them around a coffee table—there was tea in a glass kettle with flowers floating in the water, there were candles everywhere lighting up the room with care, in the most appreciative sense of the word. There was a sheen of love painted in the air and Mila felt it, along with her guilt, double. She had been misrepresenting Jakob in her mind all evening.

She settled on one of the cushions. He sat across from her.

"I'm sorry," she said.

Somehow, he already knew that she was sorry—she sensed.

"I know," he said.

They held each other's eyes a while longer than usual. She wanted to communicate everything that was in and outside of her heart—how she appreciated him more than she could let on and how his patience was soothing. She said nothing though, and hung her thoughts in the air hoping he would understand them.

misleading men arent mind readers

"I know,' he repeated.

Feeling reassured, she blinked her eyes closed, taking a sip of the warm tea.

"This is the perfect sleep-time tea, where did you get it?" she asked him.

"At the market last week," he explained, "It was called something adjacent to *Night Spell*."

Night spell, indeed, she thought, for she felt the enchantment rising in her like the heat of fire starting low and making its way up.

He blew out the candles one by one when their tea had lessened and lessened—their cups took on an empty shape, not to be pessimistic, but to imply that the act of consumption had finished and it was time to fill them up anew or to sit with the emptiness. Tea drinking is a spell for letting go of the ego, Mila thought.

She thanked him in between other words for being himself.

He kissed her, and she kissed him, and they kissed each other to make up for not having seen one another much lately. She kissed him, and he kissed her, and they kissed each other to let the other know how much they liked being pressed together. His hands held her with grips both tight and loose, and their breaths were scattered across the room as if they were confetti being thrown around in celebration of something new.

XVI.

THE SUN(DAY)

Saturday night and its obscenities had just passed—it was technically Sunday, for it was very early in the morning. Mila and Jakob were tucked into the crevices of her comforter and its engrossing, cloud-like shape determined where their limbs could intertwine—if at all. Their eyes remained closed, but sleep had not yet settled into their mouths. Their voices bounced back and forth between them—a game of verbal tennis to show that each was a worthy opponent of conversation.

Their game was interrupted by Jakob's ringtone not long into Mila's decision to fall asleep.

"Hello?" Jakob whispered.

Baz explained, all in one breath, that he had lost his keys, was slightly drunk, and that he had gotten the job.

"Tell him to just come here," Mila said, having overheard the conversation happening next to her.

Baz was at her door within minutes. She let Jakob deal with Baz's needs and settled into one side of her bed, drifting to sleep. Dreams did not disturb her and neither did the weight of Jakob getting back into bed.

A hand laying on Mila's face woke her up. She picked it up and placed it squarely away.

"Morning," she heard Baz say from the other end of the bed.

Mila turned to look at Jakob—who was sleeping in between the two of them—for an explanation. She pulled on the comforter a bit, settling into a position facing Jakob now but exposing Baz's torso to the cold chill of day.

Jakob's hand was resting on the curve of Mila's waist. She took the scene in, sinking deeper into the comfort of her bed, closing her eyes, and letting a soft sigh of pleasure escape her mouth organically.

"He's too tall for your couch," Jakob said.

"Morning," she said, stretching out the word.

Mila yawned, greeting the morning with her voice.

She had imagined Baz in her bed many times before, but never like this. She assumed this was better than any other possible scenario. Mila slipped out of bed to drink some water. She made like a sunflower and turned toward the window in her room—the sunlight was peering in slowly as if creeping up on her, turning past buildings into pockets of unobstructed spaces right into Mila's home. She smiled as the sun danced upon her face. She realized the moment was nothing less than beautiful. This was a void of her choosing—noticing the beauty of a sliver of time and feeling nostalgic for it while it occurs—for how likely is it to be repeated again, in exactly the same way? The present held an oddly abstract place in her mind—it was something to savour into the stickiest parts of her thoughts, the ones that did not understand the dangers of yearning for presence. And although it was not desire she was presently taken up with, it was a love for being alive at the right time alongside people who *are* the right place.

It couldn't have been earlier than nine in the morning, but the light gently captured the silhouette of the men cuddled in bed, not necessarily with each other, but their bodies grazing the sheets in precious stances. They seemed like little kids, one brother bearing more responsibility than the other. Their resemblance was almost symmetrical in their same coloured boxer briefs and bare chests. Mila's own sleep-clothes matched the deep blue of their bottoms.

She finally drank her water and began to braid her hair as to tuck away its consequential mess from slumber.

"How do you have so much energy right now?" Baz asked, either implying that it was far too early on a Sunday morning to have such energy, or that he was still feeling the effects of the night prior.

"I am only alive on Sundays," she—*I* said.

The words felt like a final truth, as if I had been meaning to say them all along, but there was something holding me back. It was out there now, though.

I am only alive on Sundays when the prospect of sleeping in is on the table—lazing about, sticky nectarine drips, rose-scented treats, the day of the holy, spent and in love!

I am only alive on Sundays—mesmerized by the idea of the sun freckling life.

"Saturday nights for me," Baz said.

"We know," Jakob said, slamming a pillow on his own face.

Baz and I laughed—The Tweed was back.

"What's Tweedy's day?" Baz asked.

The nickname caught Jakob's attention—he whipped his head toward Baz only to find a teasing smile there. I watched in anticipation, teetering on my feet to see if Jakob would be offended, but noticing Baz's persisting grin, he eased, realizing the joke was intimate and with no harm intended.

"It *has* to be Monday morning," I joked.

"I'll have you know, I *am* Sunday," Jakob said.

And I did know somehow, deep down. He was my type of person.

"Alright, everyone up. And someone make the bed, please," I told them.

I stood at my normal spot in the bathroom in front of the mirror—looking past myself and at the tiles in the back. Everything was alright today—the blue was pale and the sky outside was brightened by the sun. I knew I wouldn't have much time to myself, but I would spend it with two people I loved, and that was also a Sunday I could write my name all over.

Baz and Jakob joined me in the bathroom with sleep dripping from their eyes. They both stood tall, but they still looked like little boys disoriented from a car drive they had fallen asleep in. I handed Baz an extra toothbrush while Jakob and I grabbed ours; we all took turns spitting out toothpaste into the sink.

"Mila, I told Jakob already," Baz started, with his brush still in his mouth, "I got the job."

"I knew you would," I told him, "Congrats!"

Jakob smiled at us, he seemed to like that we were getting along.

"How are things with Donya?" Jakob asked, spitting out his last mouthful of toothpaste.

"*She* is definitely alive on Monday mornings," Baz said.

All of us understood what that meant, and we shuddered at the thought—perhaps a little too dramatically.

I left them in the bathroom gracing the floor of my apartment in a familiar path. Straight to the kitchen to make some coffee. I didn't know if Baz drank coffee, I had never seen him this early in the day.

"Coffee?" I yelled to them.

"Coffee," I heard both of them echo in unison.

They eventually joined me in the living room, Jakob reaching for his phone to put on a playlist I had made myself familiar with in the early of morning. I watched him fumble with the speaker cord for a bit, and although he knew what he was doing, time slowed once again with a sense of finality. The sunlight was hitting his bare back—his freckles glistened with speckles of gold. I poured out a cup of coffee for him, the colour of it filling my heart—as if it was a vessel for such things—it was a deep, warm brown I could get lost in, the way I had so many times in my own eyes in the mirror, or like Jakob's hair when it was caught in the light of a burning candle. I was contemplating Baz's hair, darker than both of ours, when I noticed he was giving me a blank stare.

"What?" I asked.

"Cold water...do you have any?" he asked.

"Oh yeah, one sec."

The irony of what was going to happen was not lost on me. I would pour water from the vase I had made to get over Baz, into a cup, for Baz to consume.

I opened the fridge door, kneeling to see onto its shelves. Immediately after reaching my hand in, another hand grazing mine startled me and I yanked it back out. I made no sound to suggest distress, and composing myself, I looked to the back of the fridge which was seemingly mirroring me. I knew the image to be Lila, of course. She was reaching into her own fridge, the colour of her shirt was the reverse of mine—a very light pink, nearly white. I could see past her into her home, and two men there, too. Though while in my home they were friendly, chatting amongst themselves, in her house they were stood up, full of anger or passion—I couldn't tell which state of being drove them to speak so loudly to one another.

Lila and I acknowledged each other, I took my vase out, and closed the door on her.

XVII.

THE EMPRESS

The day was still very young. We rested our heads on the hard floor mediated by my fluffy white carpet. Jakob hoisted his legs atop my loveseat—Baz flipped through the pages of a magazine I had laying around. The pages lingered in the air with each turn—Baz was gripping them with his index finger and the middle one at the edge of a page. The sunlight fell on his mundane task in a way that I could not look past. Jakob seemed to be nodding his head along to the music he'd chosen. And I—I was finally witness to the spectacle that is being alive. In the simple nothingness of a morning spent idling in the sweet nectar of breathing. I felt, at that moment, that life is a succulent nectarine, and my purpose is to sip it delicately; each droplet of juice acts as a symbol or sign from any and all gods to begin every day as if it was my first—to forego what I know would happen if nectar spilled onto my shirt, to simply live every day anew.

I knew opportunities of parallel play, such as this with Baz and Jakob, would be far and few, and so when my instinct for hunger started boiling over from my stomach into my mouth, I shoved it down for a while longer to savour something not entirely edible. But it was still Sunday and the market was where it always would be on a day like this.

Right on cue, as if me thinking of the market prompted the idea in either Baz or Jakob's mind, they both suggested a visit at the same time.

"You guys *are* twins," I told them with a more serious tone than I meant to.

Only Alive on Sundays

I caught a glimmer of annoyance on Jakob's face and gave him a smile to let him know I was only partly serious.

They looked at each other and shrugged—seemingly taking my sentiment as a compliment or agreeing between the two of them that I was up to something again.

My turtleneck scuffed at the skin of my neck. I wanted to reach in from above and scratch the irritation within, but it was near impossible to dig my entire hand into the high, and tight, neckline. Retrospectively, I could've picked a better garment for a chilly day with an unrelenting side of sun, but my mind was not accompanying me in the selection process. I pulled the collar outward to let some air in between my body and the hellish garment. One of my nails skimmed my throat, leaving a mark—I realized it had been a while since I'd cut them. If I were to dig them into, say, an orange here, I'd undoubtedly break its skin—the barrier between its life and death, and the juice would rush down my hands. It would be a gruesome act, one I would not partake in, but the thought occurred, and the image was poetic and it brought me to butterflies. The act would be powerful, perhaps, but namely strange. I felt that this was the trace Lila imprinted onto my psyche after our short encounter in the fridge. Was she a *short love,* too?

Baz and Jakob were trailing behind me as if I had dragged them out here, despite the trip being their idea. I eyed the market and saw the usual, but there was a smell of a long-lost home that drew me in—I was overcome with the steaming scent of cardamom, coming from none other than the tea stand. I started toward the teas and quickly realized it was a ploy on the part of the universe: for it was not the tea I was interested in on this particular day, but a new stand next to it.

It was humble in the most mysterious sense of the word. It contained a surplus of supply, but its source was not visible. There was a simple table with a girl standing behind it. I noticed her when I finally peeled my eyes from the rolls of paper tied by various coloured ribbons—some were more ransom-note looking than others.

If Donya was the dirt and trees, this girl—she was the air and sky herself. She was likely the ether incarnate.

And she worked at Luna before I took over.

"Celeste," I called out, almost incapable of holding in my excitement.

I had not seen Celeste in the years since she left the shop, despite the fact that we had grown close to one another prior to her departure. She always had a friendly demeanor but was stern at the same time. She was full-force with Luna back in the day, and I assumed I had to follow in her shoes, keeping the shop open every day of the week. Seeing her felt like coming home. She was a bygone friend somewhere in the world of transient *hello*s and *goodbye*s.

"Mila!" she shouted back.

We embraced and I felt her warmth fall onto my shoulders and back, trickling all the way down to my feet. My turtleneck sweater became unbearably itchier from the inside—it brushed against my skin as if each thread was grabbing onto a skin cell and rubbing it raw. I thought: this is exactly how it feels to hold onto something you love that doesn't quite fit right. Perhaps I made Baz feel raw—rubbing at his sore spots with the yearning I devoted to him. And, perhaps, he mistook the attention as reciprocating the feeling from time to time, and I mistook his confused responses as love almost all the time. This was the power of Celeste: every interaction with her offered some deep wisdom from myself. I always thought she was an extension of Luna, or Luna of her. Perhaps now, I could know.

"Grab a fortune first," she said, softly.

It felt as though everyone could read my mind today.

I unravelled a piece of paper from the pile marked "fortune," and it was blank. I chuckled in mock remembrance of the many I had received in the last few weeks. I turned it around to show her the paper.

"Blank," I informed her, despite its obvious lack of wording or fortune.

Celeste smiled, as if holding some truth within its crevice. I felt a similarity in her smile to Jakob's—it was always knowingly.

"From the ether," she said, "I guess," feigning ignorance.

"From the ether," I confirmed, matter-of-fact.

The normalcy of the situation took away from its novelty—so we slipped into accounting for lost time as two women who are otherwise preoccupied with jobs or thoughts would do.

"Where have you been, Celeste?" I asked, bordering on concern.

I was actually trying to hide my unquenchable desire to live as she does—so certain of the world—vicariously, of course.

She filled me in on her new courier role and the fact that she'd left Luna to make at-home deliveries from the ether. Every Sunday she'd get a new batch of letters, empty or written out, with addresses to fulfil the orders. Some would be marked with a delivery date, others relied on her to know when to step in.

"You're quite popular with the ether," she noted with a wink.

"And what's the point?" I asked, annoyed at the presence of yet another blank piece of paper intentionally void of meaning.

"No point other than to question," Celeste noted with a sigh and a hint of boredom.

"Am I right in thinking you, the ether, send these out when someone is thinking of you?"

"Yes, but it could also be a reminder to think of yourself," she filled me in nonchalantly.

She was right, I guess. Each time I had gotten a letter, I could've been prioritizing myself more. Instead, I was projecting myself into the moment, and giving it what it demanded of me instead of demanding of it, or myself, what I needed. I thought back to when I had received the giant pile of letters at home after visiting the market. It was a Sunday, and amongst the first that I had decided to keep the day open for myself—and the shop closed, also for myself. I had felt guilty having assumed the moment was asking of me to be with Luna, and then I had settled for being okay, for being with the discomfort of defying the inner laws of magical antique shops. But I could've taken it as a symbol for how I'd felt everything pile on after spending countless, continuous days at Luna. I could've used the blank pages as an opportunity to sift through each, writing my anxieties or poems onto them, and then taking the time to consider their weight. Would they have changed shape? Would they have spoken my verses and worries back to me? It's true, every time I got a letter I considered it a stern statement, a scolding maybe, from the ether. But what if, all along, it was a push to question my assumptions more. Why was the ether right in telling me to get over "it"—Baz? I knew it was a push in the right direction, or maybe just a potential, but *why*? The desire to consume this information was irritating me more than the turtleneck now.

It was suffocating.

"Why you?" I asked, knowing she was worthy of mediating between the ether and the world, but I wanted to know how she got to that point.

"The same reason it's you who runs Luna now—you saw its potential and knew you could tend to it, be part of it, help it grow."

I knew what she meant.

"Thanks," I told her.

I felt sweat beads form in the dips of my clavicles, they dripped down the narrow path from my chest to my stomach. Though this time, it wasn't because the sweater was ripping into my soul with its weight, but because Baz and Jakob were a short distance away examining some fruit. They seemed to be projections of one another, yes, and they both made me feel good, and bad, in different ways, but I knew them as extensions of me out in the world. It was me that failed to know them—really know them.

I looked back to the curiosity of Celeste's stand and was hit with my own mystery of existing. The pulsing nectarine pit locked in my ribcage slowed, glazing the encounter a hazy orange over my eyes—the whole scene was sweet but sticky from not having been slurped up all in one go. The romance sat there, as it usually did, and a swarm of flies, metaphorical, of course, nestled into the ducts of my eyes.

Maybe, now knowing this, I was cured of my tendency to long morbidly for the picturesque[11]. This was a more interesting thing about me than Jakob, or Baz, could ever be.

XVIII.

THE HANGED MAN
(OF LETTERS)

I lost Baz and Jakob momentarily at the market as I wandered off to different stalls to stock up on my produce. I gathered some pistachios, a rainbow of fruits, and some hearty vegetables—in the most figurative sense of the adjective.

I felt that fall was upon me soon, despite it having already arrived. The time spent alone inside my mind was the much-needed breeze of a summer day giving respite between sweaty skin and limbs. I felt a sense of safety with the men nearby, but was undisturbed by the typical gnawing need to see what they were up to, and if they wondered about me and what I was up to—their rattling existence was an inner orchestra of maracas in the space between my ears. They seemed to be prancing around the market from stall to stall together. Who was following who was unclear. My heart ached as if again pierced by a sword; their friendship had blossomed so seamlessly that I was sure the blood that I leaked was a green adjacent to the inside *and* outside of a kiwi—a confusing mix of love and hate. There was a different type of value in the friendship they offered each other, and I was an outsider. But, I realized, I didn't want what they had, I wanted my own version untainted by expectations of what a connection needs to look like and feel like.

We reconvened at the fountain in the middle of the market after I was finished with my alone time. The men were there eating some sunflower seeds and flicking the shells into a bag Jakob was holding up. They remained in their set of clothes from yesterday, Baz in what he had gone

Only Alive on Sundays

to the party in—jeans and a hoodie—and Jakob in jeans, a white t-shirt, and a green tweed jacket to match the tiling in his bathroom. His outfit was a hybrid of his own styling and Baz's, I presumed. I wondered if Jakob's tweed was unnerving for him the same way my sweater was.

"How about you two drop off your groceries, and Baz please rid yourself of the alcohol smell somehow, and meet back at mine this evening?" Jakob told, or asked, us.

"Yes, Tweed," I teased.

Baz held back a smile and Jakob rolled his eyes in jest.

Baz held up a bag of limes he'd purchased, "Margaritas."

He said it with such certainty that there was no space to argue.

"Yes, Tweedy," Jakob joked.

I burst out laughing—it felt as though the understudy had finally been granted the gig.

Unintentionally, the day slipped by in a more distant way than I expected it to. I was not consumed by much thought—I was simply existing at home. This is all I ever wanted, for the incessant obsessions to one day cease so that I can just sit on the couch and be. There is a danger in such activities, though—the minutes trickle into one another and one tends to forget that time is very much alive and a breathing organism that we must all agree to take care of and devout our lives to.

Checking the hour, I grabbed my hot tub essentials and phone. There was a text from Baz sent minutes prior to my jolt back into the day—he was asking me to pick up tequila. He had spelled it "tewuila." The men were drunk.

I grabbed a bottle of tequila from my cabinet and promenaded the short distance to Jakob's.

The walk over was strained by a thought—I did not know where Baz lived. He knew where I lived, but all I knew for certain was that it was in the opposite direction of my apartment from Jakob's house. I had never seen the inside of Baz's. The thought made me feel violated, in the loosest sense of the word. I felt that Baz had seen the most intimate corners of my life and home—and Jakob's—but I had not seen his. They both knew me, but I did not know them as individuals who also happened to be acquainted. Though Jakob, I also felt I did not know for a different reason—we shared secrets about our lives, but I could not make a composite image of him other than *The Tweed* or *my boyfriend*. Though, that was not his fault. A sense of guilt arrived just as I did to his house.

The lights were off and the was door unlocked; I entered following the chatter of the men to the backyard. They had music going and both of them were submerged in the hot tub, tipsy-looking. A glass was knocked over on the deck behind Jakob—ice cubes and lime slices crawled out of it. They both looked at me in silence, though expectantly.

"I have it," I told them, pulling the bottle of tequila out of my bag.

"Thank god," Jakob said.

He emphasized god, despite it being me who had brought it over.

"Thank her indeed," Baz added.

Jakob stepped out of the hot tub to make me a drink—the water dripped off him slowly, down his torso, off his shorts, onto his toes and the deck. I took him in for a second, he seemed more emboldened as he was radiating a type of heat I'd never seen on him—there was something off about him. I knew he was probably more drunk than Baz was, and so his guard was likely down, but he was either confident or arrogant, and I could not place it. I changed into my bathing suit in the bathroom while staring down Jakob's tiles—they seemed even darker in green tonight, as if matching his brooding attitude.

I dipped into the tub—its heat welcomed me in against the chilly September night. Baz was in there alone, his head resting on the deck as he sunk lower into the tub's depth. Jakob lowered himself in, too, offering me a perfectly salt-rimmed glass. He kissed me on the forehead more gently than I expected him to due to his otherwise strange demeanor.

I took a sip and noticed that Jakob's pour was heavy. My face warmed immediately—the heat of the hot tub enveloped my body while the drink heated my cheeks. The tequila dripped down my throat burning my guilt with its trail down. I gagged a little, which made Jakob smile. It was sly, mischievous, and I'd never seen this side of him despite him warning me of it in our talks. He seemed as though ready to stir the proverbial pot.

"Is this for me or you?" I asked him.

"Me," he said, "and you."

I nodded in mock understanding. I looked at Baz to see if his expression would give me a hint as to why Jakob was acting so odd, but he seemed just as confused. It was my presence that had brought this out of him, I thought.

"I got one of those fortunes," Jakob started.

"Oh, me too, at the market," Baz added, "Mine was blank though."

"Mine, too," I told them.

"Mine wasn't," Jakob said, "In fact, mine said something weird. I just read it before you got here, Mila."

"What?" I asked breathier than I meant to—my voice was abandoning me.

Baz was watching this conversation happen, and I felt him grow uncomfortable as his eyes darted away to the trees and then to the inside of Jakob's house just to avoid eye contact with either of us.

"It said to 'get over it,' whatever that means," Jakob let us know, though he was only looking at me, ignoring Baz who was now getting out of the hot tub right beside him.

"And you're mad at me because?" I asked with conviction, feeling that he was attacking me for whatever he was realizing.

He looked like he was making it known—inside himself—that his anger was displaced as he took a second to consider what to say next.

"I'm not," he said, moving across the hot tub to get closer to me.

I looked at him wanting him to go on because the irony was that I had gotten over what was in between us, and now he had to get over something. I knew it was me that had him feeling off—feeling like the deeper green offered by the outside of a watermelon.

I waited for him to say something before jumping in, but he did not.

"I got a letter like that a while ago, if it makes you feel better," I admitted.

"That does not make me feel better. What did you get over?" he said slowly, seemingly suspecting foul play.

"Baz," I told him simply, with no explanation attached to it.

"Maybe I need to get over Baz, too," he said, smiling now.

That did seem to make him feel better. I took a deep sigh.

"How do you mean?"

"I love the guy, but I feel as though he's always there. I want to be more me when I'm with you, more Tweed, but—"

"Wait," I interrupted.

This is why I didn't know him fully. He wasn't letting himself be Jakob, the real one, not this Tweed stuff I'd assigned to him and that he'd taken on, especially when

Baz was there. And second to that, *he* was always inviting Baz into our time, not me. I told him the latter.

"Oh," he said, noticing the truth in the sentiment, "I guess that is what our dynamic has become, it felt natural."

"Right. Well, I like you when we're alone, and I think we need to be alone more, Jakob."

"I," he started and took a pause, looking away from me.

I held his face with one hand. He took another sip of the margarita.

"I think a break would be better."

"A break?" I asked, confused and a little mad.

"I mean, I still want to see you, and Baz, and continue our dynamic. It works. But I believe I need to take us as a partnership out of the equation, just to see what that's like," he told me confidently.

"So you want to be friends?" I clarified.

"Yes," he confirmed.

"I don't need more friends," I told him.

"I think you might," he responded without hesitating.

It stung, but he was right. Another sword came crashing deeper into my heart—or maybe my ego or psyche—and I desperately wanted to switch my mind-TV back on. I got out of the hot tub, grabbed a towel, and walked through his house to the front door, leaving a trail of wet footsteps behind me. I put on my shoes, fully drying myself in the doorway, and pulled on a hoodie that I had brought.

I opened the door to find Baz standing there, illuminated under the streetlamp. I stared at him before fully exiting, expecting an explanation.

"I saw that heading south and wanted to stick around," he blurted out.

I closed the door behind me.

"Thank you," I told him, feeling relieved.
Baz cares about me.
"What colour are your bathroom tiles?" I asked.
"Want me to show you?"
"Yes, Basil," I let him know.

XIX.

(DON'T ACT) THE FOOL

My feet were stuck.

I had instinctively chosen *flight* at Jakob's, and *freeze* in the middle of Baz's bathroom.

I momentarily considered it one of Baz's energetic traps, but I could only credit the feeling to being allowed into his sanctuary—though I'm not sure if that's what he'd call it.

I hadn't grasped much of his decor or the layout of his house while being escorted to the bathroom. I didn't have a chance to see the colour of his couch or absorb the look of his stovetop. He rushed me into the bathroom sensing my buzzing curiosity to finally see what his soul looked like. But my feet were glued to the floor, the lights were still off, and my soles were bare. I took in the cold of the floor as if I was a tree taking in food from the earth, learning from the ground which season it is, which moment of life I'm in—if I am even alive or not. I tried to read him, to understand what he would get out of this, but all I cared about was knowing what his tiles would tell me. I had previously imagined they would be dark, maybe blue or purple to match how mysterious he could be.

His finger hovered over the light switch. I was twitching with anticipation while the moonlight leaked in from the angled skylight muffling the colour of the tiles, yet still acting as a preview. They looked too light to be a dark shade of anything. I settled for pale, like mine—they must be. They could be grey, but that would be horrific. Bathroom tiles say something about humanity—they determine someone's humanity. And we don't necessarily choose them, they choose us. How much of a neglected void would Baz's soul be if there was no blush to the walls of his bathroom, the place where people go in the waking hours of time, and then again just before the sleeping ones? Our reasons for living are coded into the rooms we occupy, the spaces we let ourselves take deep breaths in. Decorative ornaments, furniture, antiques—they can only tell you so much. Bathroom tiles—they are cryptic little symbols, signs, to decode, to make meaning of. Of all that, I was sure.

"Are you ready?" he asked in a sing-song carnival voice.

It was an unexpected break in the mostly tame way Jakob spoke. I loved how animated Baz could be, but it was as if they were the same person tip-toeing between personalities and ways of being.

"Yes! Show me," I pleaded.

He took one of my hands, squeezing it tight. The way my fingers crushed into one another made the excitement feel more visceral, I felt it in my hands, in my arms, in my entire shape.

He flicked the switch—he exposed his walls.

I looked around at first, not saying a word. I opened my eyes, closed them, blinked, closed one leaving the other open, pressed a hand into my eyes—all just to make sure I had it right.

My heart spun. I was not expecting this. I let go of his hand to explore the tiling, dragging my finger down a spot by his mirror and toothbrush. The bathroom was more organized than I expected it to be—neat, a laundry basket, containers for things that I certainly did not have containers for.

"Do you have a cleaner?" I asked, suspiciously.

I looked back at him—hands in pockets, as was usual in scenarios like this.

"No," he said, smiling, dropping his shoulders in relief.

"Interesting," I said, walking the perimeter of his bathroom, inspecting it for signs that he actually did live here.

I watched him open the mirror to reveal a cabinet behind it. There was a slight mess in there, but it was hidden away, and it made all the louder the pounding in my chest. His hands roamed the shelves in search of something—his forearm twisted and turned in ways I was forbidden from noticing before. I peeled my eyes away, taking another turn to savour his tiles. I wasn't entirely sure when I'd see them again—or Baz, or Jakob, at that.

He opened the window atop the bathroom letting in a chill I was only just getting used to this time of year. I felt goosebumps rise wildly on the back of my neck. He held out a joint and I finally eased into the night. We passed it back and forth between us, strategically standing just under the window. As my sensitivity heightened, my toes called to me from the floor—it was beginning to form a thin layer of ice on its surface, in the most realistic sense of the metaphor.

I sat at the edge of his bathtub, staring into the abyss of his tiles; the abyss likely stared right back at me[12]. I felt the air loosen up, it untied itself from some energetic knot that was placed in between Baz and I. Gravity's grip on reality took a backseat momentarily. A deep breath fell into my lungs and I closed my eyes once more.

I was in love with Baz's tiles.

They were so pale a yellow that they were almost indistinguishable from a creamy white. But, indeed, they were yellow, like the inside of a banana cocooned in the darker, more poignant, yellow of its peel. Some tiles were noticeably darker, giving a childish curiosity to the whole wall—was it on purpose, did someone set these tiles in a pattern of darker and lighter only known to themselves? Did the colours of the lighter ones just wear out over time, somehow? His yellow reminded me of the sun—not looking at it directly or observing it in any way, but the sun I imagine when I'm just waking up, getting used to reality at my feet, cozied in sheets undisturbed by my senses taking information into my mind to be processed at a later time. It was the sun on the inside—behind closed eyes. An imagining of what it might be like if I had only ever been told about it and had never seen it for myself.

"So, what do you think?" he asked, noticing my eyes were closed for a little too long.

I batted them open, this time disturbed by the amount of light in the room. I had almost forgotten he was in the bathroom with me.

"I love them," I told him, but then decided to add, "Not at all what I imagined them to be like."

"Why not?" he replied with genuine curiosity in his eyes.

I turned off the lights, he took it as a cue to hold my hand again. This time he was more gentle. His fingers wrapped around mine softly, his thumb tracing an imaginary route on the side of my hand.

"I just assumed a darker colour."

"Why?"

"You were always just a little out of reach—"

He cut me off, "I wasn't out of reach, I was always there, here. But you always expected something from me and—"

Now I cut him off, "Can you blame me? With your random hand holding and—"

"It's not random."

"Then, what is it? You just like laying a trap and then backing away?"

"It's not a trap, Camila," he said, trying to subdue his frustration.

"Then, what?" I replied, in a quiet way that sounded more like I was giving up than demanding an answer once and for all.

Was everything bound to be doomed today? I thought Lila would take me for a fool in this instance—I had the opportunity of Baz right in front of me, his hands constantly chasing mine, but I didn't leap into it. I felt angry at her, I felt like she was watching me, judging me, telling me how to be myself...or herself. I didn't even care about Baz anymore. Not like that. I missed Jakob, he was always level-headed, he never pursued anything he didn't *really* want.

"It just never felt right. I wanted to, so many times, and the timing was off, or I was in my own head, or you were with Jakob, or—"

I understood what he meant.

"It's okay," I told him.

I hadn't intended to blame him for not being able to decipher his own heart.

"Do you want to know *why* they're yellow?" he asked me.

"Of course," I reassured him, smiling.

"It's a breath of fresh air. There's this dreadful doubt that runs in my mind at all times and I can never escape its voice."

He paused, thinking the next part through.

"It's like there's an alternate me who never believes anything will go right. And my bathroom here, even though it doesn't match the rest of my place, is the break I need when I wake up from a stress dream, or come home from work after telling myself the day has been shit."

His bathroom tiles were what his soul needed, I confirmed.

"That voice isn't you," I told him.

"I know," he said, though not knowingly or convincingly, just hopefully.

I gave him a hug, holding him as tightly as he had held my hand when I was frozen just a few minutes ago.

"I love you," he said, taking pause and then finally adding, "as a person."

I was sure I loved him in the past, but I did not. I loved him now, as a person, too.

I finally knew him.

The night turned into Monday—Sunday was now in the past. I felt myself deteriorating with sleep, falling into the void of nothingness after my day spent alive. Baz must've noticed the world of dreams spilling out of my eyes because he offered for me to stay the night. I wanted to, for walking home seemed the biggest chore at hand—it was a sour nectarine which my stomach turned at the thought of— but I didn't want to like him any more than I loved him.

"I want to but—"

"But nothing, just stay."

I nodded in confirmation.

And like clockwork, I heard a letter slip into Baz's mail slot.

XX.

THE WHEEL OF FORTUNE

Today, the neighbour's tea—the scent ripe with orange peels and candied apples—broke through the walls that separate our living quarters and climbed up my nostrils. I sipped the smell with joy, pleased with the make-shift alarm clock. I had reserved this Sunday to clean and cleanse. Another day in which I am alive and the sins of the past week could be washed away.

What I really wanted was a warm drink to comfort the beginning of day bookending the cold of night. Though my cup of choice would've been coffee, none remained. I settled for the last bit of *The Love Blend*. I hated to admit, being a believer in all things enchanted, that this specific brew offered no love. I hadn't spoken to Jakob since he so abruptly ended us last week. Unintentionally, he had turned into my *short love* of the season. And as if all the minutes of *short love* I'd lived through with Baz weren't enough, the universe seemingly loved throwing more at me in different people and things.

I drank the tea—its calming rose flavour soothed the path from my lips to stomach with a warm hug. This, too, was *short love*—some acts of love would never happen if other moments of pain or pleasure didn't occur first. I wouldn't have been in Baz's bathroom standing beside him and holding hands if Jakob hadn't gotten that letter from the market. He probably wouldn't have gotten that letter if he hadn't seen me so absorbed by the stand talking with Celeste. I could blame the whole debacle on Celeste's presence, but why was she at the market in the first place? If she's the one delivering the letters to people regardless of if they want the realizations that come along with them or not, why bother putting up a stand? It is all interconnected, and we are all a witness to the happenings of energetic forces beyond humanity—I am learning, and learning to be okay with—nothing changes the fact that I still have to go through every day and manage to come out alive, not just living but alive. I have to preserve the romance of being me, living here in this now-year, knowing who I am, and doing what I do, *despite* not knowing what it means. It just has to mean something to me. And in that moment, it meant that…I had to go to the market and stock up—on coffee, on bread, on nuts, on nectarines.

Eyeing the tea stand after collecting everything else I needed, I decided that I could go for more tea. The vendor pointed out a lavender tea. I placed my eyes on it and could almost physically see the magic, the glitter I imagined to be emanating from it. The label read: *Bath for the Soul*.

I needed that.

It was an oddly pleasant day. Everything was lining up to be where I needed it to be, the market knew today was my day of cleanse and it offered exactly that. I felt relieved that there was no Celeste and no cryptic warnings. The signs had drained me.

The letter last week at Baz's was definitely an interruption that he didn't need. I had pointed out to him that I heard a letter slip in, and he had brushed it off, saying they were all too common these days. I had asked him if he knew what they meant. He had said he didn't care. I considered him brave at that moment, for he never sought to make sense of what clearly did not. He never thought a god or person was angry with him when he had no reason to. I always jumped at the opportunity to work on myself or to heal whatever the letters wanted me to, but Baz just let them be. He didn't overthink them—he didn't even think of them as a sign. It's not that he is unwilling to work on himself—rather, he is not obsessed with letting the ether tell him when or how. He's doing it on his own terms, and that was something I admired. I was learning from Baz, it seemed. Maybe that was the connection—I had to go through Jakob to see Baz for who he was and put aside my preconceptions to finally learn from him.

I considered how that equation would affect Jakob while shoveling in more of the tea into the small sachets the vendor supplied me with at a steady rate. It would be cruel to think of Jakob as a mere crutch in this situation—I had learned from him, too, but it was more than learning. I had experienced life with him. And I liked it. I could hear his voice saying *hey*, and it felt nice, warm—it was as if I had summoned him in thought, feeling enveloped by his energy. I had been avoiding even thinking about him all week, but I let him in now, and it was okay. I missed him, even if it was just as friends.

"Hey," I heard again.

I looked to my left, then slowly to my right where I was faced with Jakob.

"Can we talk?" he asked.

I wanted to, but I had just begun understanding what had happened between us.

"Sure, but not now. Do you want to stop by later?" I asked him.

I needed to be prepared. To clean and cleanse before we spoke.

"I'll see you later, then," he said—smiling, knowingly.

Always knowingly! He had continued to speak in such a reserved way ever since we first met, always offering subtle hints at what he was feeling on his face—that could very well be *his* trap. I realized he had hooked me in with his charm and he never even had to try.

At home, I quenched my thirst with water out of the vase. I had my palm on the neck of the vase, I was admiring what it offered and realized that I'd abandoned pottery once again. I hadn't been back since I got what I needed from the studio, from the act of creation—closure. Though this time, I hadn't lost myself in someone else, rather I'd found myself in the small moments of existing between the big ones. I didn't have to commit to a place to be on certain days to really know myself. It was okay to skip pottery.

I began to scrub my kitchen counters and found myself mesmerized by my arm moving rhythmically back and forth with tension to get off the grime. My muscles tensed and relaxed, revealing a once again evident shine. I cleaned the bathtub, did my laundry, and it was in those encounters that I found the divine. I found the Sunday in me. The way I moved with body and mind, allowing one to lead the other in order to make room for the new, the bright, was a spell for finding the string that connects all of life.

I began filling the bathtub as the sun started to slip down the sky—reflections of golden light were sprinkled across my tiles and the stream of water pouring into the tub. I missed Jakob's hot tub. It was a place where I let my guard down so many times—he had shown me *how* to do that—and he had also been forgiving when I put it back up.

The water trickled in slowly, I witnessed it move with grace. I decided to throw in some of the lavender flowers from my tea—its name likely planted in me the idea to take a bath, though not by any subliminal messaging but, rather, through realizing how pleasant an idea it is to bathe one's soul. I grabbed a few from the kitchen—and it was my proximity to the front door that allowed me to hear a gentle knock there. My heart mirrored its pattern, knocking in my chest like a mock imploration to enter—or escape.

I opened the door to find Jakob on the other side. I knew it would be him but was still surprised to find him there.

"Come in."

He came in, scooting his shoes off. I watched him close the door behind him, his fingers tensing and relaxing around the door handle. He felt airy, light.

Today was his day of being alive, too.

I looked at him expectantly, and he stared back blankly. I noticed him looking past me, concern filling his eyes with an urgent widening.

"Your bathroom," he said, "it's flooding."

"Oh fuck," I said, running toward the bathroom to turn off the tap.

I had the lavender flowers in one hand and threw them in less than delicately. I uncovered the drain on the tiled ground of the bathroom and let the water flow down, relieving the floor of its piled wetness. Jakob grabbed a few towels and placed them down. I went back to the bathtub, plunging my arm down to pull out the stopper so a little water could escape and make room for me when I eventually entered the tub.

"Listen," Jakob said as the chaos settled.

I sat on the ground readying myself to place the stopper back in when I saw fit. He sat on the edge of the tub atop a towel.

I looked at him expectantly again. I wanted him to lead this conversation, since he'd led the last. I would be willing to be friends, if that's what he still wanted.

"I saw you leave Baz's place Monday morning."

"Right, it's on your way to work," I added, realizing he'd made an assumption already.

"What happened?" he asked, as if he had any right to an answer.

But I *wanted* to tell him. I missed confiding in him.

"Nothing, he showed me his bathroom tiles."

That seemed to concern him more than if I would've said anything had happened between us.

"Why?" he asked, a look of sadness taking over his face.

"I wanted to know what colour they were."

"Why?" he repeated, patiently.

"I," I stopped because I didn't know how to answer, "I just wanted to know."

"What difference did it make?" he asked.

I put the stopper back in the drain.

I understood. He was asking because he had figured out what they meant to me. He knew the tiles were an *in*—that they reflected to me what people wanted out of the world, love, life—fruits of the living, nectarines! The tastes of being alive. The tiles grounded me, reminded me of our souls, how we find them in the tiny crevices of how we live our lives. The pale blue of my bathroom was a reminder to keep it light, that nothing could ever be so serious as to demand attention away from existing as I am. Lila's pale pink was more flirty, and I would imagine her's to be darker in red, but perhaps the pink was a reminder to always love, and softly at that. Jakob's dark green was brooding but fresh at the same time—as if being in a forest full of mist—it was his soul reflected in the newness of plants growing. *He* always approached every day like it was his first. He made leaps and trusted himself on the other side. And Baz's yellow tiles—the brightness he needed to know that everything would be alright. The tiles are just tiles at the end of the day and I'm sure for countless people in the world they mean nothing but, to me, they are the proverbial hearts we wear on our sleeves.

"I feel like I know him now," I admitted.

"And where does that leave us?" he asked shyly while searching for my eyes.

I wanted to go back to how things were, but I settled into the reality that things were changed.

"Friends," I said.

It was the only way to keep both him and Baz in my life—intimately close. I could see that it wasn't the answer he came here for, but it seemed that he had just accepted the fate of the situation, too.

"Good," he said, at ease, "I feel like I finally know you," he added.

I smiled, knowingly. He couldn't have known me until I did, until I figured out who I was in the world—how I related to other people existing on the same plane.

"I'd offer you a place in the tub, but it's not very spacious as you can see," I joked with him.

"We can't all be so lucky as to have lavish hot tubs," he teased back.

It was easy knowing him. I told him that.

"I can't say the same, but I'm glad I can continue knowing you," he said, and then added after I didn't say anything in return, "Your birthday is in two weeks, right?"

"It is, indeed," I informed him.

"Have any plans?"

"Not yet."

I had not even thought about entering into the next Sunday of my life.

"Okay, enjoy your bath," he said, "Baz and I shall plan something."

The idea made me quiver with a lingering sense of pleasure—I was not used to receiving such favours from *friends*.

"You guys don't have to," I let him know, "but let me know if you need anything," I added, before it seemed like I didn't want them to.

"Alright. See you later, Mila," he said, showing himself out.

I turned off the light and lit some candles, stripped my clothes off and dipped into my bathtub. My tiles glistened back a secret: I am in love. Not with anyone, but with the world, the sky, the sea, the moon, the sun, I am in love with Sundays in bed sipping nectarines. I am in love with the hours that the sun kisses, I am in love with kissing the sun. I am in love. I hope one day I'll share that love with someone outside of obsession turned *I love you as a person*, outside of *short love* turned friendship. But for now, it's me, the world, and the smile of people living life side by side—connected by a string I'll never understand—a horizon I'll never get tired of.

XXI.

THE CHARIOT (AWAITS)

I surprised myself with how long it took me to realize how pretty Baz and Jakob looked—both were poised into the loveseat at Inferno's drowning in conversation, lit warmly by the bar's incandescent state of being. This was indeed our watering hole—we came here to quench our metaphorical, and respective, thirsts. It was where ideas and relationships—and envy at times—blossomed. And right now, as I stepped into the bar having been told by both of them earlier in the day to meet them there, I could see a cloud of potentiality hovering over both of them. Each word they exchanged seemed to evaporate up to the cloud, mingle with the rest, and become something entirely different than what was originally intended. I knew they were discussing my birthday, just a week away, but the forthcoming celebration was dancing in my heart with both excitement and fear.

*

Luna had worked me to the bone on Monday, and although I felt cleansed from the string of expectations that connected me to Jakob and Baz, it had been a startling beginning to the week. Patrons were lined up and a steady flow of conversation brewed amongst them. I caught chatters of when the shop would open as I arrived not too late in the morning. I had opened the door and everyone had poured in, not slowly like a trickle of rain, but all at once like a wave in full force. They had all crashed at the shore of the portal section. I would've liked to clean the shop before anyone began tracing the intimate folds of Luna, but time did not afford me that. Instead, I had gotten to making tea, *Bath for the Soul*. I had not tried to mediate between those keen to get their hands on whatever they could and the resistance or implorations of the portal—I just let it unfold. I had watched how a man dressed for work—namely not a Tweed, but rather a Suit—thrusted himself toward a watch. It hadn't mattered to me what it meant, and I'm sure it had mattered to him even less. It had probably been a moment of distraction to fulfil whatever emotionless void he was entertaining. Perhaps to tie him to his bloodline, like I had assumed with Jakob and the painting, to give him something to make sense of life out of. A mother holding her daughter's hand had dropped it at the sight of a doll that the daughter should have been more excited for, but was not. An elderly woman had picked up some tablecloth, overjoyed by its simple presence. Everyone had been looking for a sign. People are convinced that if they can take a hint from a force greater than themselves, then everything was meant to pan out exactly the way it had. Humans are desperate creatures writhing for the opportunity to have their reality confirmed; I am no different—I had thought.

It was not that the week had been arduous or demanding much of me, but rather, I had felt indifferent. Not knowing the reasons why people were in search of memories lost to time had made me feel uneasy—it was as if we just go through the motions playing out roles like Mother Nostalgic For A Time Before Children, or Worrisome Father Who Never Had To Care For Anyone Else Before And Doesn't Know Where To Put All His Love Because He Never Learned. I further realized then that life *must* mean more, and it did when I could convince myself that others saw it too!

When people had stormed into Luna in multiples that I could not count or get to know, the magic had escaped me. Understanding patrons' motivations is what allowed me to uncover the mystery of other people, to befriend them

Only Alive on Sundays

in ways that didn't need a label—temporarily or longer. I had come to learn that from Lila, Baz, and Jakob. But it had been impossible for me to talk to so many people all at once. Luna needed more from me than I could offer. Perhaps it was time to enlist help, I had thought.

The patrons were still rummaging through the shop and I had closed my eyes, scouring the depths of my subconscious for Lila, I knew she would understand.

She had materialized behind my eyes once I called to her from within me—the echo of my voice had filled my lungs and the air had dropped deeper into my being.

"Come work here with me," I had told her while allowing her to see through my eyes the chaos that ensued when no one was there to talk the patrons through their findings.

"I have my own to deal with," she had said, allowing me to see through her eyes then.

In her version of Luna, the antiques were old, dusty, unwanted. She had been sitting in her shop with its still air, suffocating from loneliness.

"There's no one there," I had told her.

"It needs me," she had said.

She had looked as if life had slipped out of her like hair down the drain.

"Just for the day, then," I had pleaded with her.

"Fine," she had said, hesitating at first.

I had opened my eyes, releasing a breath I hadn't realized I was holding. And there she had been, turning a corner from behind the shelf of the portal section as if being introduced to an audience.

No one had batted an eye—everyone was busy with their toys. She had helped me throughout the day, gotten to know people, helped ease their tension, collected payments from right pockets despite my constant reminders to take from the left. Nothing would happen, as far as I knew, but that was how we did things at my Luna.

And then, at the end of the day, I had asked her to come to my birthday party.

*

I needed to break the news to the men at Inferno's.

"Sit, sit," Baz said, removing his coat from the single arm chair across the table from the loveseat.

I sat, sat.

"You're going to have to decide because we are unable to," Jakob told me.

"I assumed you two would've come up with the same exact idea," I informed them jokingly.

"I proposed a cocktail party, at my house—Twenties themed," Jakob said.

And I couldn't lie, I loved that idea. It was almost not me at all, but I wanted it as soon as he let the idea out into the world.

"And I proposed a Sinners party, here at Inferno's," Baz added.

I wanted that, too. I liked the darker theme, and it felt fitting since Lila would be coming. But there was no way I could choose between the two.

They both looked at me awaiting an answer with patience in their eyes. I imagined each of their hearts thumping like nectarines ready to burst with sap—all in anticipation of which I would choose.

"What if we did a Sinners cocktail party, at mine," I suggested.

They both seemed disappointed but relieved. They understood the weight my option carried. Neither won nor lost. I had unintentionally placed them in purgatory by making no real decision, despite it being the safest choice as I could choose neither, fully. One would always be tainted by the other, and the other would sour in the shadow of longing, always there to disrupt whatever could happen, though likely without ill intent. I understood their motivations, their story—how we had all gotten here.

We changed topics quickly—before I could interject. Baz spoke of his new clients, how he had kept them happy and at bay. Jakob spoke of his students, how they had finally gotten into the groove of reading and discussing the hidden layers of a book. And then, once again, they looked at me. Expecting me to recap my week, my work. And here was the perfect opportunity—the ripest nectarine for me to bite into presented itself.

"I hired someone to help out at Luna," I told them.

"Quick turn around," Baz noted.

"That's Mila," Jakob added.

It seemed somewhat backhanded, that he was somehow implying I'm quick to move on, but I knew he didn't mean it with ill will. I was reading into it because it was true. Everything had transpired between all of us so quickly—I had gone from lusting for Baz to being great friends who at times held hands, and although that was confusing, it was happening naturally. I was not forcing it to fall into place like this. I could not be blamed.

"Not me, the universe," I replied.

Like routine, a knowing smile grew on Jakob's face.

"Well, her name is Lila, she pretty much looks exactly like me, and she's coming to the party."

"Oh," they both said, catching onto something I had forgotten.

I had told them about the dream.

XXII.

THE TOWER

Sunday, my birthday, brought me to life—it rushed through my bloodstream as soon as the clock turned its back on the previous day. My apartment was brimming with people—most of which I knew, but some I did not. ~~Mila's~~ My gaze found Baz amongst the crowd of people. He stood behind my kitchen island manning the bar, making cocktails all tinted red—of which I'd had several. My blood was likely half sticky sap and half his hellish concoction now—a Sinner's Sunday. He was adorned with devil horns, and I felt like I was going to throw up. Not because of his horns though, despite how adorable that was. I was nervous for when Lila would show up. The men had reluctantly accepted that she would be present given that it was *my* birthday—it only then occurred to me that it may be her birthday, too. And so I awaited her arrival with tension between me and everyone else. Every interaction was tainted with my nervous tendency to slip out of reality. But it was officially past midnight, and having gone through the awkwardness of everyone bombarding me with birthday wishes precisely as a random day turned into a holy one, I began to make peace with the fact that she might not show up.

    Jakob startled me by standing in my line of vision and blocking out the scene I was lost in. It was not that Baz's barmanship was extraordinary or even mesmerizing, I just needed a moment to find my footing. People swarmed around ~~her and~~ us, and they seemed to morph all into one. If life were a movie, the two of us would be idled in the middle of a blur of people moving in unison, cancelling out each other's individuality. I still felt as though I could throw up—perhaps my body was picking up on what was about to unravel.

"Back on the glances, I see," Jakob said sternly.

I steadied myself by holding his shoulder. His lips looked more plump than ever, almost like they were delicious, forbidden fruit. I recognized what he meant after getting lost in the universe of his face momentarily. He was talking about Baz.

"Jealous, are we?" I said back to him, raising my eyebrow.

He took me by both shoulders—suddenly the floor felt more sturdy, flat—I stared at him. I was calm, collected.

"Yes," he said, "you could be a little more subtle, you know."

I smiled, unknowingly. I was not even looking at Baz with lust or a desire to fall under him at this time of night, but it seemed that Jakob was settled on it.

"I'm not *trying* to look at either of you in a certain way, you know that right?"

"It's just him you look at," he said doubtlessly.

I took his hand and led him through the path of people parting at my presence—*happy birthday*s were thrown in along the way and I caught them all with a smile but couldn't grasp onto a single face attached to the words.

"Baz," I tried to assert, though it sounded more like a question, "Do I look at Jakob in a certain way?"

He laughed. I watched his eyes drop down, but more so droop down, to our hands. I let Jakob's hand go and the ground beneath me re-adjusted itself into a tilt.

"Yes."

I looked at Jakob to make a point out of it, a silent *I told you so*. He did not look calm and collected like me.

"Then, stop," Jakob said.

"You want me to stop looking at you guys?" I asked to confirm that he really did just say that.

"No, no," he admitted, shaking his head.

I had not even noticed what they wore today, or how their smiles looked to say the same little secret, or anything else like that. And I was about to say as much when ~~Mila~~ I noticed someone out of the corner of my eye that looked to be Lila. But upon turning my head to get a better view, I realized it was a mirror that I had peripherally caught my own reflection in.

I turned my attention back to Baz and Jakob, who had both started talking about something else at this point. Baz was making Jakob a drink. A nectarine pit started turning itself in the very bottom of my gut. I felt bad to have picked a fight where there wasn't one. My eyes tend to linger, and although I drove pleasure from that at times, it should not matter to either of them where I look. Baz never mentioned it because he knew it was just a look. Jakob—he took it for more.

"Can you guys meet me in the bathroom in a few minutes? I just need quiet for a second and then we'll talk," I asked them.

They both nodded.

I tried to follow the trail I had a million times before, kitchen to bathroom. Simple. But I kept getting stuck in between people—my friends from university and from the pottery studio, and Celeste, they were all there—and though we'd all talked already, each wanted to stop me and talk more. And I wanted to talk, too, to people that weren't Baz and Jakob, but I needed a second to collect myself first.

Why the possibility of Lila coming unnerved me, I did not understand. I had seen her many times; we were even on good terms now. But she was a threat—her presence here would override mine somehow. Everyone would want to know who she is and why we look the same.

Only Alive on Sundays

Maybe Baz and Jakob would be more interested in her than me. Maybe one would take to her, and I'd have the other to myself. The potential of that was not something I actually wanted. I would always be jealous of her version of things—not because I was missing out or because my version was particularly bad, but because there would be another me living adjacent to me doing things *differently* than I would be. It would be a nightmare to see how things *could* pan out based on differently made decisions. It was fine in another reality, but in this now-here, there was only room for me. It was unsettling, and I now hoped she wouldn't show up—I had a desire to get rid of some sort of excess in my life, to throw out a set of rules I felt I'd been given by the ether—that I *had* to live by. I was jealous of who I *could* be and, clearly, not at all calm or collected.

I barged into my own bathroom and locked the door behind me. The tiles were paler than ever; as was I in the mirror. I stuck my head down the toilet. Breakfast, lunch, and dinner leapt out of me and floated in the bowl—then, down they spiraled after I pulled the trigger on the flush. I sat at the edge of my bathtub, the tiles glistened with the haze of a pleasant day—an easy blue sky, children running in a meadow, perhaps a kite floating in the wind. The tiles were calming, collecting.

The doorknob rattled—it was time to explain myself. To tell the men that I was sorry, that I was flirting with the line between friendship and more without intention.

I opened the door and found only one person standing there. I hurried her in.

"Party's almost over," I told her.

"Sorry! I got caught up with work."

"It's your birthday, too, isn't it, Lila?"

"Yes," she said, "but I didn't have much planned."

The jealousy I felt moments ago evaporated out of me. I noticed her disposition, her loneliness, and though I had felt it before, too, I now liked how I'd handled it. I like who I am—I'm distinct from other versions of me who have lived under different circumstances, I thought.

"I want to introduce you to my Baz and my Jakob," I said.

They knocked on the door just then and I quickly ushered them in. Their lips were painted a dark red and it seemed as if they had drunk the blood of night in my short absence from the party. They had momentarily drained me dry of desire, but it came rushing back—not desire for them, but for a final leap into not desiring at all, to be free, to no longer be split in two.

We all stood there; no one said a word.

"This is Lila," I told them.

They looked at each other. I looked at Lila.

"Who is Lila?" Baz asked.

"She is," I said, confused.

Jakob walked toward me. He held me by the shoulders once again; the floor finally adjusted itself to lay flat beneath my feet.

"There's just me, Jakob, and you in here, Mila," Baz said.

I looked at Lila in the mirror, her pink bathroom tiles, and my own blue ones around the mirror. I gripped the amulet from Luna I'd decided to wear to my party and felt it pulse in my hand; it was warm and somehow alive, beating—I had considered it to be a part of the shop, but maybe it was a part of me and only at the shop because I was. I held Lila's eyes watching how we morphed into one. It was as if we were interjected by time and our realities were just now collapsing. There was no need to hear how she would carry on—we would live inside one another, always there for the communing, but never disturbing the way things are. It was a momentary blip on my part to invite her *out* into my life.

"Oh," I said.

Jakob let go of my shoulders. I took my seat on the ledge of the bathtub again. Baz sat beside me and Jakob took a seat on the floor.

"I'm sorry, guys," I started, but said nothing after.

There was nothing to say. My mind had played a trick on me to make the point loud and clear.

"Happy birthday," Baz said, giving me a hug.

I felt the rhythm of his heart pump into mine as he held me chest to chest.

"Thank you," I said.

"Happy birthday," Jakob said, opening his arms from his spot on the floor.

I went to him and sat in front of him with his arms wrapped around me.

His heart spoke in whispers into my ear—I pressed it against his chest harder.

"Shall we?" Baz asked, standing up.

"Let's," I said.

He helped me up first. Then, offered his hand to Jakob.

"Tweedy?"

Jakob took it.

The three of us vacated the bathroom to find that most people had already left. Only a select few were staggering in a circle, discussing something, or nothing, of interest. Their eyes turned toward us, and I assumed we looked guilty—I appeared slightly disheveled—because they averted them as fast as they had glanced over and began placing their drinks down to reach for their coats at the door.

Murmurs of *thanks for having us* filled the living room and the door was shut behind them, leaving just the men, myself, and a mess to clean up—during the waking hours, of course.

"You guys okay to sleep on the couches?" I asked.

And despite their monstrous height in comparison to the length of my loveseats, they nodded in agreement.

"Just throw us some pillows," Jakob added.

I gave them everything they needed, nearly tucking them in, and entered my room to write myself a letter for the next half-decade. I knew the previous letter said something about falling in love being the goal, and I had surpassed it a million and one times over. It likely also said something about Baz—I, however, did not want to read that now.

I began writing the new one. It somehow felt like I was addressing it to Lila, hoping to make herself, but actually myself, understand how the last three months had unravelled. I wanted to speak objectively, to put distance between facts and feelings, and I would, but there'd be more to it. Everything that happens is mediated by my predispositions, feelings, biases, and experiences. I wanted to tell the story from my perspective. The loves I endured, the pain and the pleasure—all with my own name written on them.

I penned away in my moonlit bed. The night was quiet and the smell of a party—of people who spoke over each other and kissed in hallways—still remained in the corners as if they were marked territory.

My eyes caught a gift sitting atop my nightstand. It was a rectangle wrapped in newspaper with a little bow on top—very clearly a book. I undid the wrapping to find Oscar Wilde's *The Importance of Being Earnest* and two cards—one from the bookshop and another from Jakob:

I like knowing you. Happy birthday, Camila.

That's it. That's all he'd signed it with. It was an interesting choice of literature to gift me, but I nonetheless hugged it to my chest. He did know me.

Only Alive on Sundays

The card to the bookshop was none other than the one from his left pocket when we first mocked the ambiguity of being strangers. I now understood it to be an epilogue to our relationship: the *Three of Swords*—a heartache without blood, as if the swords pierced into the heart prevent a disastrous leakage much greater than the pain of being stabbed in the first place.

I still had not returned to that bookshop. I'd need a new journal after finishing this one out, a new one dedicated to the year ahead of me. I could stop by tomorrow, albeit a Monday, and pick up a new one, perhaps it would be the perfect place to find something to house my vices and verses.

I put the book back on the nightstand and, beside it, noticed a plump, soft temptress begging for my lips—a nectarine. The light of the moon highlighted its dents and subtle curves. I traced its silhouette, its shadow on my wall—I held it up to the moon and demanded its secrets be unveiled any time now—soon. I bit into it, keeping my mouth ajar with its presence. My teeth held the nectarine in place with my lips parted to keep it still. The juice dripped down my neck, but I did not bother to wipe it off; the truth of a nectarine is sticky, it would be senseless to strip it of its defining quality. I continued my letter with the taste of a finished year still in my mouth, but also with another one just ahead, and with clarity on my mind.

My hand flopped around my drawer in search of something with answers.

I unraveled the cloth around my tarot deck, shuffling it very slowly to steady the tension in my mouth holding the nectarine in place.

The Moon flew out, landing atop my open journal.

I took the bite out of the fruit finally, releasing my own toothy grip into it. I chewed on its flesh, devouring its sweetness after the night's mostly sour remnants. The amulet was dangling over the notebook and the tarot card, my one hand was occupied by the nectarine, the other by my pen. The scene was rather poetic, I imagined. Baz and Jakob were giggling about something or another in the next room—it sounded like a beating heart, that of my home, our friendship—it was proof that it was Sunday, and I was alive—not just living, but alive.

> *My summer—I—was jump started by tacit glances of lust and I tripped into autumn with the same look in my eyes, but I was more alive each Sunday that I gave love a try.*

THE MOON.	STRENGTH.	JUDGEMENT.	THE HIGH PRIESTESS.	DEATH.
THE WORLD.	THE DEVIL.	THE MAGICIAN.	TEMPERANCE.	THE STAR.
THE EMPEROR.	JUSTICE.	THE HERMIT.	THE HIEROPHANT.	THE LOVERS.
THE SUN.	THE EMPRESS.	THE HANGED MAN.	THE FOOL.	WHEEL of FORTUNE.
THE CHARIOT.	THE TOWER.			

A Note from the Author

This novella is a love letter—in the broadest sense of the term. But I am sure you already know. It is a celebration of life and creativity, lust and lessons, pain and pleasure, nectarines and love. The human experience in all its twisted tastes and turns—fates and that for which one yearns.

I fell deeply into this little world with its small cast of characters right after writing the very first chapter. The anticipation for what would happen next nearly always tempted me to write what I *wanted* to happen next. But there was a strategy to the telling of this story, and I want to share that with you.

I used tarot cards to move the plot forward.

I also used tarot to determine the motivations of the characters. Where Jakob is *The Fool*, Baz is the *Nine of Swords*. And to indulge you, Mila is the *Queen of Cups*—driven forward by the search for the constantly beautiful and, at times, hauntingly mundane aspects of life.

If you are familiar with tarot, and specifically the major arcana, you'll have noticed that in this book they do not appear in order from *The Fool* to *The World*. I believe that there is no real order to life, that things don't happen in accumulation of days passing by—rather, there is a randomness which we must make sense of. We could wake up one day and find ourselves in the midst of *The Star* with hope and a sense of renewal, and then see that the next day we are *The Magician* ready to create with our new-found resources—and, perhaps, we'll find ourselves in *The Tower* the week after and realize that what happened the week prior was mere practice for what's to come. This chaos that

I have observed in the world *is* the reason that the chapters unravel in no particular order. During each writing session, I would pull a card from the major arcana of the *Golden Art Nouveau* tarot deck and base the story on the greater archetypes of the card—and sometimes their divinatory meanings. *Seventy-Eight Degrees of Wisdom* by Rachel Pollack was a holy text for me while writing. I would consult each card of the major arcana with Pollack's wisdom and interpretation and add in my own understanding of how the card would play out in reality. Hence, there was always something unusual, or abstract, for me to come back to in the story. I decided to play with the wording in the card names to offer some relief, or to clue you, dear reader, in on how *I* felt about the chapter. At times, the titles are me speaking directly to you.

    Tarot is a significant part of my life. I believe it mirrors back to us our deepest desires, secrets, motivations, and can push us in the direction of alignment, healing, creativity, and connection. If you're familiar with my poetry book *Fortunate,* you'll know that I tend to spin the cards in a positive way—I always see the light at the end of the tunnel. We can blame that on me being a romantic, but I don't think there is any other way I could exist in a world full of meaning to be made. Noticing the romance of the everyday—the artistry of bathroom tiles, the enveloping smell of coffee, the welcoming material of a couch, the juice of (at times forbidden) fruits tempting humanity to indulge in our birthright—all of it keeps me attuned to love. I hope this novella works as the subtle reminder I intended it to be: find the romance, and the romance will find you.

—Kimmy

Acknowledgements

Thank you to Flor Ana for being with me during every step of the process from editing the work to supporting the idea and the book. Thank you to Athena Edwards for the feedback. I appreciate all of your efforts—this book would not be possible without you. Thank you, reader, for spending some time with me between these sheets.

And thank you, mom, for initiating me into the world of tarot.

Notes

[1] This quotation comes from the text on the *Judgement* tarot card in Rachel Pollack's *Seventy-Eight Degrees of Wisdom*. In its full context, it reads: "In modern physics we learn that scientific investigation can never form an exact picture of reality because the observer is always a part of the universe that he or she is observing. In the same way, each person's thoughts about and perceptions of life are influenced by that person's past experience."

[2] From the Shakespeare play *As You Like it*:

All the world's a stage,
And all the men and women merely Players;
They have their exits and their entrances.

[3] There's this idea in Clarice Lispector's novella *An Apprenticeship or The Book of Pleasures* that "we ought to live despite." The character Ulisses goes on to say: "Despite, we should eat. Despite, we should love. Despite, we should die. It's often this despite that spurs us on."

[4] The idiom "the world is your oyster" comes from Shakespeare's play *The Merry Wives of Windsor*—it implies that obtaining exactly what one desires can take force (or violence) at times—but ultimately, it is for the *taking* and not simply for the receiving:

Falstaff: I will not lend thee a penny.
Pistol: Why then the world's mine oyster, Which I with sword will open.

[5] From John Milton's *Comus,* a masque in praise of chastity. In this spectacle, the lustful character of Comus kidnaps a lady and tries to seduce her, offering the lines:

What hath night to do with sleep?
Night hath better sweets to prove

[6] From *Seventy-Eight Degrees of Wisdom* on *The Star* card. Rachel Pollack says: "It is one function of being a physical creature that we take this energy and use it to make poems, paintings and tapestries. All these human creations are symbolized in those several streams of water. Every act of creation objectifies spiritual energy in the thing created."

[7] From *The Star* card in *Seventy-Eight Degrees of Wisdom*: "Though the streams and the ibis imply the uses of creative energy, the experience of the Star is one of peace. For the moment, the journey can wait."

[8] From the title of Hans Christian Andersen's folktale *The Emperor's New Clothes.* In this story, two scammers fool the king into thinking an "invisible" outfit is of utmost royalty and worthy of praise. Despite the citizens noticing that the king is naked, they don't question it in fear of being reprimanded—until a child points out the truth. As an idiom, "The Emperor has no clothes" refers to something widely accepted without being criticized.

[9] From Dante's *Inferno,* Canto 3: "they yearn for what they fear for."

[10] From various lines in T.S. Elliott's *The Love Song of J. Alfred Prufrock:*

Let us go then, you and I,
When the evening is spread out against the sky
*
Time for you and time for me,
And time yet for a hundred indecisions,
And for a hundred visions and revisions,
Before the taking of a toast and tea

[11] From the popularly quoted lines of *The Secret History* by Donna Tart: "Does such a thing as 'the fatal flaw,' that showy dark crack running down the middle of a life, exist outside literature? I used to think it didn't. Now I think it does. And I think that mine is this: a morbid longing for the picturesque at all costs."

[12] From Friedrich Nietzsche in *Beyond Good and Evil:* "Battle not with monsters, lest ye become a monster, and if you gaze into the abyss, the abyss gazes also into you."

ONLY ALIVE ON SUNDAYS

copyright © 2025 by Kim Rashidi. All rights reserved. No part of this book may be used or reproduced in any manner whatsoever without written permission except in the case of reprints in the context of reviews.

Modern Portal Publishing
kimrashidi.com

ISBN: 978-1-7387720-0-1

Editor: Flor Ana Mireles
Cover photograph: *Girl at Home* by Kim Rashidi, 2023

Made in the USA
Middletown, DE
22 September 2025